ANNE MO

C000057933

DEATH AND THE DUT

ANNE Morice, *née* Felicity Shaw, was born in Kent in 1916.

Her mother Muriel Rose was the natural daughter of Rebecca Gould and Charles Morice. Muriel Rose married a Kentish doctor, and they had a daughter, Elizabeth. Muriel Rose's three later daughters—Angela, Felicity and Yvonne—were fathered by playwright Frederick Lonsdale.

Felicity's older sister Angela became an actress, married actor and theatrical agent Robin Fox, and produced England's Fox acting dynasty, including her sons Edward and James and grandchildren Laurence, Jack, Emilia and Freddie.

Felicity went to work in the office of the GPO Film Unit. There Felicity met and married documentarian Alexander Shaw. They had three children and lived in various countries.

Felicity wrote two well-received novels in the 1950's, but did not publish again until successfully launching her Tessa Crichton mystery series in 1970, buying a house in Hambleden, near Henley-on-Thames, on the proceeds. Her last novel was published a year after her death at the age of seventy-three on May 18th, 1989.

BY ANNE MORICE
and available from Dean Street Press

ANNE MORICE

DEATH AND THE
DUTIFUL DAUGHTER

With an introduction and afterword by
Curtis Evans

DEAN STREET PRESS

INTRODUCTION

By 1970 the Golden Age of detective fiction, which had dawned in splendor a half-century earlier in 1920, seemingly had sunk into shadow like the sun at eventide. There were still a few old bodies from those early, glittering days who practiced the fine art of finely clued murder, to be sure, but in most cases the hands of those murderously talented individuals were growing increasingly infirm. Queen of Crime Agatha Christie, now eighty years old, retained her bestselling status around the world, but surely no one could have deluded herself into thinking that the novel *Passenger to Frankfurt*, the author's 1970 "Christie for Christmas" (which publishers for want of a better word dubbed "an Extravaganza") was prime Christie—or, indeed, anything remotely close to it. Similarly, two other old crime masters, Americans John Dickson Carr and Ellery Queen (comparative striplings in their sixties), both published detective novels that year, but both books were notably weak efforts on their parts. Agatha Christie's American counterpart in terms of work productivity and worldwide sales, Erle Stanley Gardner, creator of Perry Mason, published nothing at all that year, having passed away in March at the age of eighty. Admittedly such old-timers as Rex Stout, Ngaio Marsh, Michael Innes and Gladys Mitchell were still playing the game with some of their old élan, but in truth their glory days had fallen behind them as well. Others, like Margery Allingham and John Street, had died within the last few years or, like Anthony Gilbert, Nicholas Blake, Leo Bruce and Christopher Bush, soon would expire or become debilitated. Decidedly in 1970—a year which saw the trials of the Manson family and the Chicago Seven, assorted bombings, kidnappings and plane hijackings by such terroristic entities as the Weathermen, the Red Army, the PLO and the FLQ, the American invasion of Cambodia and the Kent State shootings and the drug overdose deaths of Jimi Hendrix and Janis Joplin—leisure readers now more than ever stood in need of the intelligent escapism which classic crime fiction provided. Yet the old order in crime fiction, like that in world politics and society, seemed irrevocably to be washing away in a bloody tide of violent anarchy and all round uncouthness.

Or was it? Old values have a way of persisting. Even as the generation which produced the glorious detective fiction of the Golden Age finally began exiting the crime scene, a new generation of younger puzzle adepts had arisen, not to take the esteemed places of their elders, but to contribute their own worthy efforts to the rarefied field of fair play murder. Among these writers were P.D. James, Ruth Rendell, Emma Lathen, Patricia Moyes, H.R.F. Keating, Catherine Aird, Joyce Porter, Margaret Yorke, Elizabeth Lemarchand, Reginald Hill, Peter Lovesey and the author whom you are perusing now, Anne Morice (1916-1989). Morice, who like Yorke, Lovesey and Hill debuted as a mystery writer in 1970, was lavishly welcomed by critics in the United Kingdom (she was not published in the United States until 1974) upon the publication of her first mystery, *Death in the Grand Manor*, which suggestively and anachronistically was subtitled not an "extravaganza," but a novel of detection. Fittingly the book was lauded by no less than seemingly permanently retired Golden Age stalwarts Edmund Crispin and Francis Iles (aka Anthony Berkeley Cox). Crispin deemed Morice's debut puzzler "a charming whodunit . . . full of unforced buoyance" and prescribed it as a "remedy for existentialist gloom," while Iles, who would pass away at the age of seventy-seven less than six months after penning his review, found the novel a "most attractive lightweight," adding enthusiastically: "[E]ntertainingly written, it provides a modern version of the classical type of detective story. I was much taken with the cheerful young narrator . . . and I think most readers will feel the same way. Warmly recommended." Similarly, Maurice Richardson, who, although not a crime writer, had reviewed crime fiction for decades at the *London Observer*, lavished praise upon Morice's maiden mystery: "Entrancingly fresh and lively whodunit. . . . Excellent dialogue. . . . Much superior to the average effort to lighten the detective story."

With such a critical sendoff, it is no surprise that Anne Morice's crime fiction took flight on the wings of its bracing mirth. Over the next two decades twenty-five Anne Morice mysteries were published (the last of them posthumously), at the rate of one or two year. Twenty-three of these concerned the investigations of Tessa Crichton, a charming young actress who always manages to cross paths with murder, while two, written at the end of her career, detail cases of Detective Superintendent "Tubby" Wiseman. In 1976 Morice along with Margaret Yorke was chosen to become a member of Britain's prestigious Detection Club, preceding Ruth Rendell by a year, while in the 1980s her books were included in Bantam's superlative paperback "Murder Most British" series, which included luminaries from both present and past like Rendell, Yorke, Margery Allingham, Patricia Wentworth, Christianna Brand,

Elizabeth Ferrars, Catherine Aird, Margaret Erskine, Marian Babson, Dorothy Simpson, June Thomson and last, but most certainly not least, the Queen of Crime herself, Agatha Christie. In 1974, when Morice's fifth Tessa Crichton detective novel, *Death of a Dutiful Daughter*, was picked up in the United States, the author's work again was received with acclaim, with reviewers emphasizing the author's cozy traditionalism (though the term "cozy" had not then come into common use in reference to traditional English and American mysteries). In his notice of Morice's *Death of a Wedding Guest* (1976), "Newgate Callendar" (aka classical music critic Harold C. Schoenberg), Seventies crime fiction reviewer for the *New York Times Book Review*, observed that "Morice is a traditionalist, and she has no surprises [in terms of subject matter] in her latest book. What she does have, as always, is a bright and amusing style . . . [and] a general air of sophisticated writing." Perhaps a couple of reviews from Middle America—where intense Anglophilia, the dogmatic pronouncements of Raymond Chandler and Edmund Wilson notwithstanding, still ran rampant among mystery readers—best indicate the cozy criminal appeal of Anne Morice:

> Anne Morice . . . acquired me as a fan when I read her "Death and the Dutiful Daughter." In this new novel, she did not disappoint me. The same appealing female detective, Tessa Crichton, solves the mysteries on her own, which is surprising in view of the fact that Tessa is actually not a detective, but a film actress. Tessa just seems to be at places where a murder occurs, and at the most unlikely places at that . . . this time at a

garden fete on the estate of a millionaire tycoon.
. . . The plot is well constructed; I must confess
that I, like the police, had my suspect all picked
out too. I was "dead" wrong (if you will excuse the
expression) because my suspect was also murdered
before not too many pages turned. . . . This is not
a blood-curdling, chilling mystery; it is amusing
and light, but Miss Morice writes in a polished and
intelligent manner, providing pleasure and entertainment. (Rose Levine Isaacson, review of *Death
of a Heavenly Twin, Jackson Mississippi Clar-
ion-Ledger*, 18 August 1974)

I like English mysteries because the victims
are always rotten people who deserve to die. Anne
Morice, like Ngaio Marsh et al., writes tongue in
cheek but with great care. It is always a joy to
read English at its glorious best. (Sally Edwards,
"Ever-So British, This Tale," review of *Killing with
Kindness, Charlotte North Carolina Observer*, 10
April 1975)

While it is true that Anne Morice's mysteries most
frequently take place at country villages and estates,
surely the quintessence of modern cozy mystery settings,
there is a pleasing tartness to Tessa's narration and the
brittle, epigrammatic dialogue which reminds me of the
Golden Age Crime Queens (particularly Ngaio Marsh)
and, to part from mystery for a moment, English playwright Noel Coward. Morice's books may be cozy but they
most certainly are not cloying, nor are the sentiments
which the characters express invariably "traditional." The
author avoids any traces of soppiness or sentimentality
and has a knack for clever turns of phrase which is char-

acteristic of the bright young things of the Twenties and Thirties, the decades of her own youth. "Sackcloth and ashes would have been overdressing for the mood I had sunk into by then," Tessa reflects at one point in the novel *Death in the Grand Manor*. Never fear, however: nothing, not even the odd murder or two, keeps Tessa down in the dumps for long; and invariably she finds herself back on the trail of murder most foul, to the consternation of her handsome, debonair husband, Inspector Robin Price of Scotland Yard (whom she meets in the first novel in the series and has married by the second), and the exasperation of her amusingly eccentric and indolent playwright cousin, Toby Crichton, both of whom feature in almost all of the Tessa Crichton novels. Murder may not lastingly mar Tessa's equanimity, but she certainly takes her detection seriously.

Three decades now having passed since Anne Morice's crime novels were in print, fans of British mystery in both its classic and cozy forms should derive much pleasure in discovering (or rediscovering) her work in these new Dean Street Press editions and thereby passing time once again in that pleasant fictional English world where death affords us not emotional disturbance and distress but enjoyable and intelligent diversion.

Curtis Evans

I

(i)

THANKS to a miraculous intervention of Providence, Robin declared himself able and willing to represent us both at the funeral of our illustrious old friend, Maud Stirling, which was to be held at Storhampton Parish Church on Saturday, 13th August. The reason, as he explained to me at breakfast on Thursday morning, was that he was already committed to spending the next few days in that neighbourhood, having been delegated to lend a helping hand to the Dedley C.I.D. They, it appeared, had run into some kind of tangle which required the assistance of Scotland Yard to unravel and, since Robin had served his apprenticeship at Dedley and was closely acquainted with the terrain and many of its inhabitants, the task had naturally fallen to him.

'In fact,' he went on, 'I was about to suggest your joining me for the weekend. I saw us making a sentimental pilgrimage round all the old haunts. A funeral doesn't quite fit in with that idyllic picture, but I suppose it can't be helped. You don't mean to go yourself, though? No, very sensible. There's sure to be some stylish memorial service in London later on, which will be much more in your line.'

'Yes, but I feel that one of us ought to put in an appearance, seeing how kind poor old Maudie was to us. If you can go, it means I can sit with Betsy during the service. She sounded pretty distraught when she was telling me the news on the telephone just now.'

'Betsy not going to the funeral either?'

'Can't face it apparently.'

'Ah! The tragedy queen act in full spate, no doubt. She's stretching it a bit though, isn't she? After all, Maud must have been ninety, if she was a day.'

'No, only eighty-two; and I don't see why that should make it any easier. If you've been dominated by your mother for over half a century, I should imagine her departure would create an even bigger vacuum, Betsy's the last person to find any quick ways of filling it. On the other hand . . .'

'What?' he asked, buttering himself a fresh slice of toast.

'Nothing, really. I got the impression from the way she was carrying on that there was something else on her mind as well, but perhaps I imagined it. What time are you leaving?'

'Any minute. The car is picking me up at nine-thirty, so I'd better go and fling some things in a suitcase.'

'It's a pity you can't put it off till tomorrow, Robin, because then I could come with you. The trouble is that I've promised to auction a teapot at the South Wimbledon Summer Antiques Fair. It's in aid of some charity and they're trying to rope in as many pros as they can. However obscure,' I added, for form's sake.

'If it were just myself,' Robin said civilly, removing himself and the breakfast tray from my bed as he spoke, 'I would cheerfully wait around until every teapot in London had come under your hammer, but the Yard have this idea that since a murder has been committed it might be as well to push on a bit.'

'So it's murder, is it?' I asked, following him into his dressing-room. 'What sort?'

'Some young lady getting herself strangled on her way home from a dance.'

'Oh, one of those!'

'No, on the contrary, not one of those. Otherwise, would I be needed? This one has the hallmarks of something a trifle more subtle than the usual drunken assault or lurking sex maniac. For one thing, she was a respectably married woman who knew her way around, by all accounts. Oh damn! I'll need a dark suit now, won't I?'

'No, much too hot for that. The one you're wearing will do beautifully. Besides, it's to be strictly private. Family only, Betsy told me, apart from ourselves, and they'll all be far too busy polishing up their own images to notice what anyone else is wearing. What was her husband doing, letting her walk home alone from the dance? Or wasn't she alone?'

'Those are some of the questions I am going there to ask,' he replied, frowning abstractedly at the row of suits in his cupboard. 'And I'd be ever so obliged if you'd shut up for two minutes and let me concentrate on my packing.'

I counted slowly and silently to a hundred and twenty and then switched to a new tack:

'You'll stay with Toby?'

'No.'

'Why not? He'd love it.'

'It's kind of you to say so, but I don't believe in mixing business with relatives, even cousins by marriage. Furthermore, Roakes Common is a good half hour's drive from Dedley and I prefer to be on the spot. I shall make do with the Red Lion, which happens to be the spot, par excellence.'

'In what way?'

'It was the scene of the Saturday night dance which ended so disastrously for one of the guests.'

'You do surprise me. I should have thought Masonic dinners were more in their line.'

'So would I, but as I told you there are several unexpected features about this case. I only hope I don't run into too many more when I get there.'

'Well, cheer up, darling. I'll be down myself tomorrow evening and I'll be able to give you a hand.'

'Thanks for the warning,' he said, snapping the suitcase shut. 'I can see I shall have to work fast.'

(ii)

Unhampered by restrictions on cousinhood and with no desire to immure myself in the Red Lion, which had been craftily constructed to exclude every shaft of sunlight from its cavernous interior, I telephoned Roakes Common 3206 and invited myself for the weekend.

Toby's response bordered on the rapturous:

'You can come if you like,' he said. 'In fact, I don't mind if you do.'

'You sound a bit glum,' I told him.

'To put it bluntly, I never felt more like singing the blues.'

'I hope that doesn't mean you've got someone horrible staying with you?'

'No, quite alone. That's part of the trouble.'

'What about Ellen?' I asked. The reference was to his daughter, then aged sixteen, but already a practised soother of sore-headed bears.

'Some misguided friends have taken her to Tunisia, if you know where that is.'

'Roughly. So what's the trouble?'

'I'll explain when I see you,' he replied. 'Between nine and twelve a.m. these walls have ears.'

I interpreted this as a warning that Mrs Parkes was in the vicinity, flapping her duster and alert with every fibre of her being for his next words; so, turning to a safer subject, I said:

'Sad about old Maudie, isn't it?'

'Not particularly. She must have been a hundred and five.'

'Only eighty-two.'

'We all have to go some time,' he reminded me.

'Still, it's the end of an era, as you might say. A great international prima donna . . . last link with Melba and Caruso . . . all that.'

'Stop playing the fool, Tessa. You don't know the first thing about opera. You've been getting your information from the obituaries and they omit to mention that she was a vindictive old harridan, with a grossly inflated reputation, who went on inflicting herself on audiences long after she'd lost what voice she'd ever had.'

Since Maud had not sung a note in public for twenty years and had been acclaimed by slightly more qualified judges than himself as one of the great sopranos of the century, he had no justification whatever for these remarks. However, it reminded me that very early in his career he had written the libretto for a contemporary opera which Maud, already past her peak, had misguidedly consented to appear in. The whole enterprise had been a flop from start to finish but Maud had come out of it with a reputation considerably less tarnished than Toby's and the scarifying reviews which his contribution had received had no doubt left their indelible mark. It had been my intention to proceed in tactful stages to the proposal of his accompanying Robin to the funeral, but these recollections stayed my hand and, when I had bludgeoned him into putting a reserve of five pounds on the teapot, I told him I would be down in time for dinner and rang off.

II

DRIVING down to Storhampton was like flicking back through the early chapters of a favourite novel, for the town and its surrounding hills had formed the backdrop for my first meetings with Robin and memories of those romantic days came flooding back. Moreover, it was at Storhampton, before Robin's promotion and transfer to Scotland Yard, that we had spent the first year of our marriage and this had come about through the generosity of Maud Stirling.

Soon after the war she had acquired, among other residences scattered around in various parts of the world, an immense Victorian riverside house, originally the Rectory, and had insisted on turning over the gardener's cottage to Robin and me. The garden by then had become the sole charge of a blond and well-scrubbed Belgian named Albert, who was also Maudie's chauffeur and butler. He and a nameless individual referred to as Albert's wife, who was also the cook, were housed on the top floor of the Rectory, which had been made into a self-contained flat.

Under Maudie's lavish and indefatigable supervision, the gardener's cottage had been transformed into a bijou residence of reasonable comfort and abundant quaint charm, which we enjoyed rent free with a regular supply of Albert's wife's hot dinners thrown in. All she asked in return was unquestioning devotion, unstinted time, and a fair amount of errand running which, in my veneration for one of the world's foremost operatic stars, I was only too happy to contribute. Luckily Robin was so overworked at this period and so rarely at home that his occasional reluctance to worship at the Stirling shrine usually passed unnoticed.

On Friday afternoon I was affectionately greeted at the front door by Betsy Craig, Maudie's daughter by her first husband, who was reputed to have been killed in the 1914 war. She was a dumpy, dowdy-looking woman, who had inherited none of her mother's fabulous looks except her beautiful auburn hair; though unlike Maudie's, which had stayed beautifully auburn until the day of her death, Betsy's had faded to a dull biscuit colour, effortlessly merging through her sandy complexion down to the shapeless fawn skirt and cardigan in which she was habitually dressed.

Her full name was Elisabeth, her birth having occurred not many months after Maud's triumphant debut in *Roberto Devereux*, but Betsy was infinitely more suited to her cosy, rather old-maidish charm. Toby had once told me that she had suffered a tormented childhood in which periods of banishment to the attic, with a succession of cruel nurses, had alternated with passing fancies on her mother's part to bring her downstairs, dressed as a Reynolds angel, to dance and recite to the assembled guests. If true, it might well be a pattern of upbringing which should be more generally adopted, for no one could have outclassed the adult Betsy in filial devotion. She had willingly dedicated most of her life to the care of her mother, even to the extent of prevailing on her husband Jasper Craig, who was a documentary film director specialising in rather arty films about English landscape, to forsake his chosen world and make his home in the converted stables of the Rectory.

She was also a saint, in my opinion, unable to see ill in anyone; although Robin, no slur caster by nature, took a sterner view, holding her unvarying benevolence to be largely a pretence. Perhaps it was mainly her affection for myself and the fact that she alone of all her family had never shown resentment or suspicion of Maudie's patronage of us which chiefly endeared her to me, but I would gladly have plied her with any amount of unquestioning devotion, errand running, etcetera if it had ever occurred to her to ask for them.

'Come in, my duck,' she said, giving me a friendly hug, and then led the way to the morning-room. This, along with the office next door and the two principal bedrooms and bathrooms above, was a relatively new addition to the house and, unlike the original Victorian structure, had windows facing towards the river. The morning-room windows gave on to a flagged terrace and beyond it was a gently sloping lawn, with the bobbed tops of the willow trees in the distance, curving away from the churchyard wall, which was just visible on the right of this picture.

Betsy explained that she was not using any of the other downstairs rooms at present because there was no one to look after them. Poor Albert was so grief-stricken as to be hardly fit for work and, to crown everything, his wife had taken advantage of the general confusion to gather up Maud's best mink coat and elope to Devonshire with the local tobacconist. This was the kind of improbable situation which was always occurring in that household and I could think of nothing more pertinent to ask than:

'Why Devonshire?'

'I really couldn't say, my pet,' Betsy replied. 'Perhaps she thought it would be more sheltered there. I daresay she found this very damp and chilly after Belgium. I can quite sympathise. Poor darling Mamma could fill and warm the whole house just with her presence, but it feels like such a gloomy old barracks now. Still, we're nice and cosy here, aren't we, chick? And it's lovely to see you. Sit down and we'll have a cup of tea together. Would you like that?'

At the mention of tea, a silent and monumental cat descended from the writing desk, where it had been posed like one of Landseer's lions on the blotter, and took up a slightly more alert stance by Betsy's legs. There were always several of these four-legged bolsters dozing or prowling about in various parts of the house although with the fine Stirling disregard for names as a means of identification they were all known as Puss, with some roughly distinguished prefix: Ginger Puss, Wicked Puss, Young Puss, etcetera. They reminded me of characters from the *Forsyte Saga*.

'Tea would be lovely,' I said. 'But why don't we go and talk in the kitchen while you make it?'

'No, no, my dove, we've got everything here,' she explained, bringing out an electric kettle and battery of tea things from a cupboard by the fireplace. 'All except milk, but you won't mind lemon for once, will you? I can't face milk just at present. It goes off so quickly in this weather, doesn't it? But you can have some delicious bread and honey. Kind old Mr New used to send us such a lot when Mamma was ill. It's from his own bees. I felt like throwing it all away, to be frank with you,' she added, pausing at this point to mop her eyes with a large brown and white handkerchief, 'but one mustn't be sentimental, must one? Waste not, want not is my motto, whatever Margot may say.'

'What does Margot say?' I asked in some astonishment, for the phrase was one which hitherto I had particularly associated with her.

Margot Roche was Betsy's half sister, some ten years younger, and she had been named after the Faust heroine. She was the offspring of Maudie's second, more publicised marriage to Richard Travers, the actor, with whom, despite a fair number of intervening husbands and lovers, Maudie had remained close friends and who was a frequent visitor at The Rectory.

I had never much cared for Margot, who was an autocratic snob as well as cheese paring, with all the Stirling looks but little of the charm. She was a widow with two sons, of whom Digby, the younger and unmarried one, lived with her in a rather stylish flat in Lowndes Square, for which it was generally assumed that Maudie paid most of the rent and upkeep. Certainly the boys could have contributed nothing, because Digby, having recently left school, had joined a folk music group which nobody had ever heard of except a few other folk music groups; and Piers, the elder son, besides being married to a demanding and extravagant wife, eked out a modest living as one of numerous contributors to a popular daily gossip column.

'What does Margot say?' I asked again, when Betsy had finished mopping up.

'You'd be surprised, my darling, I'm sure you would. I confess it shook me too, but Margot has a lot more feeling than people give her credit for. She was absolutely broken up by Mamma's death. I'm sure I shall never forget her face when I have to break the news. And then, you know what she did? She went round Mamma's bedroom like some demented creature, gathering up all the little personal things she'd been using and threw them away. It was so odd, but she said she couldn't bear to set eyes on them with Mamma gone.'

'You amaze me.'

'I know, it was strange, wasn't it? But she said it was like when the boys went back to school, only worse of course. She even threw away the book which I'd been reading aloud to Mamma when she felt well enough and the empty tumbler which had had her milk in it. She simply couldn't tolerate it being washed up and used again by someone else. She even took away Mamma's spectacles. "Whatever are you doing?" I said to her. "Some old person might be glad of those. The frames, anyway," but she wouldn't listen. She just whipped them all up and threw them in the dustbin. It just shows that grief takes different people different ways, I suppose.'

'So Margot was here when Maud died?'

'Yes, they'd all arrived that evening. All five of them, even Sophie. It was lucky really, because we weren't expecting it to happen so soon. I mean, Dr Macintosh had warned us that the end might come at any moment, but we hadn't any reason to think she was worse, if you see what I mean. Quite lucid and cheerful all that day, Wednesday it was. In fact I went off to my Family Planning meeting just as usual, never dreaming the end was so near. And later on she was so thrilled to see Margot and the others. They'd been racing at Newbury, so it quite suited them to come on here for dinner afterwards.'

'And they all stayed the night?'

'Oh no, darling, only Margot. Dickie and the boys and Sophie drove back to London as soon as they'd had their dinner. Sophie said she wasn't feeling very well, I remember, and Piers thought he'd better get her home nice and early. But Margot decided to spend the night and you can just imagine what a blessing it was to have her here the next morning. All those ghastly arrangements that have to be made! Dear old Jas did his best, of course, but it's not really in his line and I can't imagine how we'd ever have got through without Margot.'

She was sniffling into the handkerchief again and, in an attempt to lead her on to happier themes, I said:

'Imagine Digby going to a race-meeting! Doesn't it rather reek of the dreaded establishment?'

'Yes, I'm sure it does, my duck, but he didn't go, you see. There's a group of young people all living on rice and doing their own weaving somewhere in the Cotswolds, and Digby and his friends went down there to take part in some music festival. The others picked him up in Reading, on their way over here. Poor Digby, he means well, I'm sure, but it must be a rather trying phase for Margot. Still, he's a dear, sweet boy and utterly devoted to his mother, so he's sure to snap out of it and get a proper job soon. Piers is a darling too. He was wonderful to Mamma during those last weeks, and often found time to come down and see her, which I thought was really unselfish of him. She got so cross sometimes, you know, about being ill and having to stay in bed. All that sort of thing was so foreign to her, and she couldn't even read for very long without getting tired. But Piers was so clever about thinking up little ways to amuse her. Once when he came he brought a tape-recorder and he said that whenever she felt in a reminiscent mood she was to switch it on and just talk about anything that came into her head. It was so perceptive of him because the iller she got the more she used to dwell on the past. Of course some of it got mixed up with the present too, but never mind. It kept her happy for hours.'

'What became of all the tapes?' I asked, for it had occurred to me that dear, kind Piers might have had a secondary motive in mind.

Betsy bent down and applied herself to the teapot. When she had refilled it with hot water and fussed and fiddled about for a bit she straightened up, handing me my cup and saying:

'To tell you the truth, my love, I've put them away in a safe place. You'll say I'm an old silly, but I was a bit worried about anyone outside the family . . . Well, the fact is, darling, there were times when poor Mamma wasn't perfectly clear in her head and she said some rather outrageous things. Just rambling on, you know, but some of it was, well . . . you know, what certain unkind people might call libellous. Piers shall have all the tapes back if he wants them, naturally, but I wouldn't care for anyone else to get their hands on them, and if he forgets all about it, well so much the better.'

I was privately of the opinion that it was most unlikely that he would, but the conversation was brought to an end by the telephone ringing. Betsy picked it up and said in cautious, noncommittal tones:

'Storhampton one three nine . . . Yes. Oh, hallo darling, yes thank you, and you?'

She looked up and mouthed the word 'Margot' at me, and I nodded and stood up. Whereupon she flapped her free hand frantically to indicate that I should sit down again but I ignored it and wandered over to the window. Sure enough, the voice inside the telephone went crackling on without pause for another four or five minutes. I strolled out on to the terrace, noticing that the vine, which was a twenty-year-old offshoot of the one at Hampton Court, had grown another twelve or fifteen feet since I had last seen it and was now spreading sideways along the balcony above. I stood for a few more minutes, admiring the empty, placid view and nibbling from a bunch of grapes just within reach and, when I turned and went back inside, Betsy was saying:

'Yes, darling, I do understand, but could we leave it for a moment? Dear little Tessa's here, keeping me company, but she has to go now, so would it be all right if I called you back in just a tick? Yes, of course I will, I'm only going to see her off . . . Yes, promise . . . yes, I will. Goodbye for the moment then. Yes, Margot . . . goodbye.'

'Poor Margot,' she said, taking my arm as we walked out to the vast and hideous mock-Jacobean hall, 'she gets in such a stew over trifles. Now she's complaining about being snowed under with letters. Well, we all are, of course. I can't bring myself to open half of them, but Margot wants to put some kind of announcement in the *Times* about answering them all personally in due course, and so on. I can't see that it matters, myself. People are bound to realise what the situation is. But you know Margot! It relieves her feelings a bit to run about getting everything cut and dried.'

Albert was crossing the hall, with a red thermos in his hand, making for the staircase. When he saw us he paused with his foot on the bottom step. His imperturbable manner and crisp white jacket had both wilted considerably under the strain of his double loss and he looked crumpled, red-eyed and faintly seedy.

Betsy, glancing up at him, instantly tightened her grip on my arm and stumbled up against me. Caught unawares, I temporarily lost my own balance and lurched sideways. We must have presented a ludicrous spectacle but there was no mirth in Betsy's voice as she called out:

'Where are you going, Albert?'

'Just taking this up to your bedroom, madam.'

He withdrew his foot from the stair and moved hesitantly towards us. 'It's rather early, I know, madam, but I've made it nice and hot for you, and I was hoping I might have the evening to myself, if you've no objection. I've left some dinner for you and Mr Craig on trays in the kitchen. I hope that will be all right?'

'Yes, of course, my dear, but where did you find the thermos? I thought it was missing?'

'No, only rolled under the bed, madam. No damage and I've given it a good wash. Did I do something wrong?' he stammered, for Betsy was still staring at him in rather a demented fashion and her arm within mine had begun to tremble. Then, evidently making a supreme effort to sound natural, she drew in her breath and said:

'No, nothing wrong, Albert. It was sweet of you to go to all that trouble. I'm sorry if I sounded sharp but we're all a little bit upset, aren't we? You go along upstairs now and try to get a good night's sleep. I'll see you in the morning.' Instead of obeying, Albert moved nearer to us, a puzzled, slightly apprehensive expression on his face, but before he could speak Betsy stretched out her hand and patted his arm.

'Run along and do as I say, Albert, there's a good boy. I'm going to have an early night myself, and there's nothing to worry about. I'll see you in the morning,' she said again, turning her back on him and steering me firmly towards the front door.

*

She stood beside my car, which had the hood down, and commented on the amount of luggage on the back seat.

'Yes, I know, Betsy, but one never knows what one may be in for in the country.'

'I suppose that's true.'

'What time would you like me here tomorrow?'

'As early as you can manage, my pet. The service is at twelve, but they'll all be coming down from London and I'm afraid there'll be a terrible lot to do, especially as we can't really count on Albert.'

As I have already indicated, I would gladly have turned cartwheels all the way to Penzance for Betsy's sake, but I was reminded that she did, after all, have a husband who might have been expected to provide a shoulder to lean on, if not some practical help in this emergency and, with my hand already on the ignition key, I said:

'By the way, how's Jasper bearing up?'

She jumped back, as though expecting me to run over her foot, then laughed in a shamefaced way at her own nerviness.

'He's all right, thank you, my duck, but you know Jas. He hasn't much time or patience to spare for sentiment. I think he's taken the punt out to get one or two shots. Very sensible, really. Much better than sitting around moping.'

These remarks, though not by normal standards particularly harsh, came as near to adverse criticism as I had ever heard Betsy deliver on anyone, let alone the cherished Jasper, and one way and another I had much food for thought as I covered the last eight miles up the hill to Roakes Common.

III

(i)

'WHERE'S my teapot?' Toby demanded, when I ran him to earth in his favourite bolt-hole, a revolving summerhouse as far away from the house as ingenuity could place it.

'Sold to the lady in the pink petal hat for fifteen-fifty. You're well out of it, really. It was fairly hideous.'

'Indeed? That wasn't your story yesterday.'

'Well, all in a good cause. You're very snug in here, I must say,' I went on, sinking into a chintzy garden chair. 'Who are you hiding from at the moment?'

'My new neighbour,' he replied sadly.

'You're surely not telling me that the Manor House has been sold again?'

The Manor was the grandest of the five houses grouped around this section of the Common and the nearest to Toby's own. It had recently been acquired by a firm of farm machinery manufacturers, a very popular development with both Toby and Mr Parkes the gardener, since it provided one with unlimited expert advice whenever the lawn-mower took a fit in its head and the other with blessed peace and quiet from Friday to Monday, when the experts were elsewhere engaged.

Toby shook his head but, being neurotically superstitious, wrapped both hands round the wooden arms of his chair.

'Who, then? Oh dear, I hope darling old Miss Davenport isn't dead?'

The properties in that small community, hemmed in as it was on all sides by Forestry Commissions, National Trusts, etcetera, all with their ever-watchful custodians, were so greatly prized by their owners that death was the only cause that sprang to mind for one of them changing hands.

Toby considered the question. 'I don't think so. At least, not noticeably deader than she ever was. No, the Griswolds have sold White Gables and gone to live in Portugal.'

'Whatever for?'

'You may well ask. Sylvia said that she must have sun, sun, sun, and that her soul was shrivelling away for lack of it, but we know better, I daresay.'

'You mean that dreary old tax thing?'

'Though what they could be saving up for in Portugal, apart from their own funerals, is rather a puzzle. Why do we keep harping on death?'

'It's in the air, I suppose. I've just been with Betsy Craig.'

'Ah yes. How was she? Talked you into a stupor, no doubt?'

'No, rather subdued for her.'

'Well, that must have made a nice change. Let's hope the effects of her bereavement don't wear off too fast.'

This uncharitable remark naturally prompted me to rush to Betsy's defence, and furthermore I was bursting to tell someone about the recent events at the Rectory, but Toby was not exactly the soul of discretion and I was determined to restrain myself until Robin and I were alone. Knowing the speed with which Toby could undermine such resolutions, I said quickly:

'Tell me, though, who's bought White Gables?'

'Well, you may picture my relief when Sylvia announced, in her whimsical fashion, that they'd sold the dear old home to a sweet little white-haired widow lady, minus dogs and children. It sounded safe enough. In fact, I was given the impression that the only faint risk was that this frail old person might be gathered by the angels before she was able to sign the title deeds, but I should have known that Sylvia would stab me in the back.'

'I suppose you should, but how did she manage it?'

'Simply by omitting to mention that the creature has white hair because that happens to be the colour she chooses to dye it, and if she's really a widow I can only suppose that her husband died from sheer desperation. She has twice as much vitality as you and I put together and she's even more stupid than Sylvia was.'

'Oh well,' I said soothingly, 'it doesn't sound as though you had much to worry about. She probably leads a very full life, so she won't have much time for you.'

'You couldn't be more mistaken. Like so many stupid people, Sylvia was arch cunning and she knew exactly what this harridan was after. She bamboozled her into buying that tasteless house by throwing me in as bait.'

'Well, really!'

'I'm not joking. Not content with spinning all those fairy tales for my benefit, she had the effrontery to describe me to this predatory female as a crusty old bachelor, too shy and proud to admit how lonely he was, and absolutely potty about the fair sex.'

'Honestly, Toby, I can't believe it. Not even Sylvia would use such language! And how could you be a crusty old bachelor with a fully grown daughter on the premises?'

'Crusty old divorcé then. It amounts to the same thing, and you can see what a farcical situation it has landed me in.'

'Very trying, I agree, but no doubt you'll weather the storm, as you have before. What's her name?'

'How should I know?' he asked impatiently. 'Jackson or something. She has told me to call her Lulu, which is not a thing one would be likely to forget in a hurry, but the only thing that need really concern us about her name is that she's hell bent on changing it.'

'Yes, I see. Quite a worry for you, but we'll think of something. And here comes Robin! Perhaps he'll have some bright ideas about how to get you off the hook.'

'He might give me some tips on how to commit the perfect murder,' Toby said, brightening a little at the prospect. 'It begins to seem like the only way out.'

(ii)

The telephone rang during dinner but Toby ignored it, explaining that people who rang up between eight and nine p.m. were hardly ever those with whom he found himself en rapport.

Mrs Parkes did not share this prejudice. She tripped in, wearing a pink nylon overall and the highest of heels, to announce that Mrs Jameson had phoned to say that all the downstairs lights at White Gables had fused, and the electric couldn't send till the morning. She was doing the best she could with candles, but the telly was off too and she'd be ever so grateful if Mr Crichton could go across and have a look-see.

To my amazement, Toby instructed her to convey the news that he would call in half an hour. Since he didn't know a fuse-box from a tennis racket, I regarded this as somewhat sinister and wondered if Ellen had given sufficient weight to the question of returning from Tunisia to find a little white-haired stepmother installed at the head of the table.

As soon as we were alone, Robin and I adjourned to the drawing-room, where he began to tell me about his case. They had pretty well fixed on the husband as the culprit, but had none of the sort of proof which the Director of Public Prosecutions would require and were now faced with the probably long-drawn-out, possibly hopeless task of waiting for their suspect to make a false move. He only spoke of these matters in general terms, however, and I have to confess that I paid them no more than token attention. I was in such a fever of impatience to bring him up to date with events at the Rectory that I seized upon the first lull to launch into a resumé of these, and asked him what he made of them.

'I don't know,' he replied, looking rather baffled by this abrupt switch of topics. 'Hadn't you better tell me first what you make of them?'

'Well, to start with, Betsy is obviously convinced that her mother died rather ahead of the appointed time, due to the fact that someone had laced her last drink of milk.'

'Ah!'

'Yes, but the point is, why should anyone bother to do that when she was due to die at any moment from natural causes? What probably scares Betsy, and I must say I sympathise, is that the milk must have been intended for her, and only got passed on to Maud by accident.'

Robin was rocking back and forth, his head buried in his hands, and his voice came out rather muffled.

'So I suppose the guilty party must either have been Margot, who afterwards went round destroying all the evidence, or else Albert, who removed the thermos in order to scrub it clean, and then pretended it had been under the bed all the time?'

'Precisely. You are brilliant, Robin! Everything does seem to point to one or other of those two, and I only wish I could decide which.'

'As I see it,' Robin said, taking his hands away from his face and speaking very seriously, 'your best bet is to confront them both with it; in private, of course, so that the other doesn't overhear. Say you know perfectly well that they murdered Maud, even though it wasn't intentional, and you'd be glad to hear what they intend to do about it.'

'Well, I'm not sure . . .' I began doubtfully, and then realised to my horror and disgust that he was sending me up.

'I'm awfully sorry, Tessa, truly I am,' he spluttered through the gasping paroxysms, 'but you are so funny. Honestly, one can't help loving you sometimes.'

'I fail to see what I have said that is so hilarious,' I said stuffily.

'Well, just because circumstances prevent your involving yourself in this case of mine, you have to go and manufacture one of your own. It's not fair to laugh, but can't you see that everything you've told me has a perfectly innocent and straightforward explanation? Oh, in a normal household, I grant you, the behaviour might appear slightly exaggerated but with that set of extrovert show-offs it's just the kind of carry-on I would have expected.'

'Albert's not an extroverted show-off,' I reminded him.

'No? I wouldn't be too sure. He may not have started life as one, but I think he became infected by the atmosphere, just like all the rest. I always suspected that perfect English butler act had a dash of the histrionics in it, and it certainly seems to have broken up pretty quickly under stress. I really believe, you know, that he got quite a kick out of seeing himself as a kind of modern Admirable Crichton.'

'Are you talking about me?' Toby asked, entering the room at this point. 'How nice! Well, I may not be very modern, but at least I managed to plunge the other half of White Gables into total darkness, so that should teach her.'

I deplored his accomplishing the business so speedily, feeling certain that another few minutes would have been enough to persuade Robin to take my misgivings seriously but he said that he had a pile of notes to go through before he went to bed and, if all were now quiet in Lovers Lane, he would be on his way.

I went as far as the gate with him and he asked me about the funeral arrangements and what time I intended to leave in the morning. I told him that I planned to be at the Rectory by ten, but he said that he would probably go directly to the church at midday, unless of course I were to need assistance with any more murders which might have taken place during the night. He then roared merrily away up the stony track leaving me no time for the blistering retort, even if I had been able to think of one.

IV

(i)

IN A sense it was one up to Robin that Jasper Craig should have been so deep in the lordly detached mood when I was plunged into my weird little interview with him on Saturday morning.

Although his work was confined to art and nature films, completed at the rate of about one every two years and made largely for his own amusement, he had become word perfect in the bohemian artist rôle, no doubt revealing himself to be one of the principal victims

of the larger-than-life atmosphere, which Maudie gener-
ated in her immediate circle. He made a cult of going
around at all times and on all occasions in the dirtiest
of blue jeans, with frayed, greyish tennis sandals on his
feet, and his thick black hair was worn long in front, so
that a heavy lock was always falling over his eyes, to be
pushed impatiently back by his nervous, sensitive fingers.
He despised what he called bourgeois chatter and spent
most of his spare time in the local pubs, where, as he
explained, were to be found the few really genuine people
of his acquaintance, a predilection which can only have
been based on the attraction of opposites.

Nevertheless it was not hard to see why Betsy's infatu-
ation had smouldered on for over twenty years, for he
possessed good looks as well as a rather perverse charm.
His features were of classical regularity, with a mouth
which looked as though it had been sculpted on to his
face and large dark, insolent eyes, which he used to great
effect. He was the kind of man who could make love to
a woman from the other side of a room, and although I
knew him to be selfish, lazy and malicious, I often annoyed
myself by finding him rather attractive.

Furthermore not even shrewd old Maudie had been
immune to his insidious charm, for she had indulged him
in every way, even going to vast expense to fit out one
whole block of the stables as a laboratory and cutting-
rooms, although this had never prevented him from
spreading all his equipment over any other part of the
house whenever he felt the urge.

Despite his somewhat unsavoury reputation where
women were concerned, I have to admit that he never
tried to exercise his charms on me, which had doubtless
contributed its share to the easy relationship I enjoyed

with Betsy. Generally speaking, he let it be understood that he was too engrossed in loftier matters to notice the existence of a ninny like myself, but this Saturday morning was the exception.

We had met in the hall as I arrived, and without troubling to procure my consent he took my arm and propelled me towards the morning-room, explaining that Betsy was in the pantry, coping with a forest of wreaths and bouquets which, in defiance of the published instructions, had been arriving at the house since daybreak.

'I ought to go and help her,' I said.

'Yes, you must, but sit down for a minute first. I want to talk to you.'

He had walked over to a table by the window and was pouring himself a drink. 'Want one?'

I shook my head. 'I'm not here to enjoy myself.'

'Very well, my little prig, but five minutes won't make any difference. I want your opinion about Betsy. You know her as well as anybody. Does anything strike you?'

'In what way?'

'Worried? Nervous? On edge? Delete what does not apply.'

'Well, I suppose they all apply, up to a point; but why not? Apart from the fact that she was dotty about Maud, there's a hell of a lot to do in a situation like this, and no doubt the rest of the family are leaving everything to her, just as they always do.'

'Including me, I suppose?'

'You're the worst of the lot, but I was thinking mainly of Margot. It's so unfair really, because in some ways . . .'

'What?'

'I often suspected that, in spite of Betsy being so good to her, Maudie secretly loved Margot best.'

'Oh, you did, did you? Nevertheless, it's not Betsy who's jealous of her bloody sister. That boot's on the other foot, isn't it?'

'Well,' I agreed cautiously, 'perhaps so, but it's a question of temperament, don't you think? Margot always wants to be first in everything. She has come to regard it as her natural place.'

'True,' he replied, getting up to fetch himself another drink. 'It's one of the things which has always made her such a great old bore, but it's only recently that I've begun to wonder whether she isn't becoming slightly unbalanced. What I'd like to hear from you, Miss T. Crichton, in strict confidence, is whether you entertain the possibility that Margot has become a trifle batty in her middle age?'

For some unknown reason, he was evidently sounding me out, but Robin's laughter still burned my ears, cautioning me not to read too much into the question. It was always possible that Jasper, bored and resentful at being edged out of the limelight, was trying to capture a little attention by mixing things a bit. It was a trick he had frequently been known to play.

'I haven't seen her for months,' I replied, having given due thought to my answer, 'so my opinion wouldn't help. Betsy told me she'd reacted rather over-emotionally, but then you have to remember that Betsy herself is slightly overwrought just now and probably apt to exaggerate trifles. It's only to be expected. After all, she's been through a gruelling time.'

'Has she? How, pray?'

'Oh, don't be stupid, Jasper. I mean, her mother being ill for months on end and then dying and everything. Naturally Betsy's been at full stretch.'

'The trouble with little people like you,' he informed me patronisingly, 'is that you interpret everything according to a set of well-thumbed rules, regardless of whether they apply or not. The truth is that Betsy's had it a damn sight easier than at any time since our marriage. She's moved in over here, for one thing, and I come for all my meals when it suits me, so she hasn't even had to make a pretence of housekeeping. Until Albert's wife skipped out, the house was running on oiled wheels, and in many ways Maud was far less bother as an invalid, anchored to her bed, than when she was creating havoc all through the house.'

'All the same, invalids can be very demanding too. They can't be left on their own, for one thing.'

'Which is precisely why there were two nurses in constant attendance; night and day.'

This raised another question which had been bothering me and I said:

'Was there a nurse with her on the night she died?'

'Oh, as to that, I couldn't say,' he replied carelessly. 'There was undoubtedly one on the premises, but unfortunately my mother-in-law had a phobia about their sitting up with her in her room. Of course Betsy gave in to her, as usual, and they'd rigged up some kind of camp-bed on the landing. The point I'm trying to get through to you is that there was someone within call twenty-four hours a day and absolutely no cause for Betsy to interfere at all.'

'Interfere? What a funny word!'

'How else could you describe her popping in and out every two seconds to see if her mother needed anything? It was Betsy who needed something, you may as well know. She needed to be needed. It's quite a worry, now that the needer-in-chief is no longer with us.'

'Cheer up! I daresay you'll still need her?'

'Oh, indeed. Though perhaps not enough to satisfy that voracious appetite. My needs are shamefully simple, I fear. So what's to become of poor Betsy? It must be so frustrating to be one of Nature's doormats, with no one around to wipe their feet on you.'

'There's still Margot, don't forget. She's an expert trampler. Is she here, by the way?'

'I believe so,' he replied, looking vaguely around, so that for an awful moment I thought he meant she was in the room. 'Upstairs, putting on her black crêpe and feathers, I dare say. Did you know that Margot was once on the stage?'

'No.'

'Well, her career only lasted for two and a half hours, so you can't be blamed for your ignorance. Probably long before you were born too, but it seems she was quite a proud beauty in her youth.'

'I can believe that.'

'What may surprise you, however, is that she considered herself God's gift to the theatre. She chalked up a few weeks at RADA and then they talked some luna-tic into putting up the money for a revival of *Mary Rose*, with Margot in the name part, believe it or not.'

'What happened? Disaster, I suppose?'

'It beggars description. She was so appalling that when she came on to take her call the gallery rose to its feet and booed her with one voice. Whereupon she collapsed on the stage in hysterics and they had to bring the curtain down in rather a hurry.'

'How curious! All the years I've known Betsy and she's never once mentioned it. But then, she wouldn't, would she, being her? And it's not exactly the kind of story which Maud would have been likely to boast about. All the same, I don't quite see what it has to do with the present situation?'

'Nothing whatever. It's just that I find it rather funny, in view of her snooty attitude to the theatre nowadays. And it always amuses me to know what made the grapes turn sour. However you're quite right, as it happens. Margot is going to make a beautiful cross for Betsy to bear. In fact, she's started already.'

'Really?'

'She's come up with the insane idea of using Maud's capital to convert this ghastly manse into flats. The plan is that Betsy and I should live in one of them, as kind of glorified caretakers, the others to be let furnished at vast profits which they would share between them. Isn't that typical? We have all the work and worry and Margot walks away with half the lolly.'

'On the other hand you'd be living rent free, I suppose, and you couldn't possibly want to keep the whole place going just for the two of you.'

'Oh, quite; but that's not the only alternative, is it? Personally, I'd infinitely prefer to sell the dreadful place, lock, stock and stables, and use Betsy's share to buy a cottage somewhere on our own.'

'And what's to prevent you, if Betsy wants that too?

Margot can't force you to fall in with her schemes. I take it from all this that everything has been divided up between them?'

'So I believe. I forget the details, but I understand that's the essence of the matter. It doesn't bother me, as you may imagine. I'm ashamed to say I don't share the universal passion for material possessions. Food and shelter and the chance to work without interruption are about the extent of my worldly ambitions, I'm afraid.'

Jasper's denigration of his own virtues was one of his least endearing habits and one, moreover, in which he was liable to become somewhat repetitive, so I got up, saying it was high time I went and gave Betsy a hand.

'Yes, you run along and do that,' he said graciously, picking up a book as he spoke.

(ii)

The pantry was a glorified passage, separating the hall from the kitchen, and Betsy was there with her younger nephew, Digby Roche. The perennial dun-coloured outfit had been replaced by a grey and white tweed skirt which I had not seen before and a black pullover which did quite a lot to light up the lingering reddish tints in her hair. One could hardly repress the feeling that it was a pity that funerals did not occur more frequently in the family.

There were two heavy, old-fashioned dressers facing each other against opposite walls and Betsy stood at one, a pile of cards in her hand, reading out names and addresses. Digby, hunched over the shelf of the other, laboriously copied them down in an exercise book. He was making such heavy weather of this task and writing in so squiggly and cramped a hand as to give the impression that it was the first time for many years that he had actually put pen to paper. He was an unprepossessing youth in many respects, having inherited the family colouring but none of its distinction or charm, and the advantages which Nature had withheld were in no way compensated for by the fact that he had recently acquired a long, mothy moustache and taken to puffing his hair up into a red gold haystack.

'Ah, there you are, my dearest duck!' Betsy said with a perceptible note of relief. 'Would you be an angel and take over, while I give Albert a hand? So naughty of people to send flowers when we asked them not to, but I think we ought to make a note of everyone who did, before the cards get thrown out. Most of them are from very old friends and I know they'll be hurt if we don't acknowledge them.'

'Dunno why you bother,' Digby mumbled. 'Why not, you know, send the whole lot round to the hospital and forget about it?'

Betsy sighed. 'I know; that's Margot's idea, but I expect the poor nurses have quite enough to cope with, without having a lot of extra flowers dumped on them. Still, if you don't feel like carrying on, I'm sure Tessa will take over, and perhaps you could do something about organising the cars? They're parked all over the drive and Mr Pettigrew will be arriving quite soon. It's most important to keep a clear space for him by the front door. Could you see to that for me, Digby darling?'

'Yeah, okay, but I better see how Mum's getting on. She might need some help too.'

'Yes, how thoughtful of you! Very likely she does, but you won't forget about the cars, will you, dearie? I particularly don't want Piers and Sophie driving in and leaving no space for poor Mr Pettigrew, even if Sophie is pregnant.'

'Still pregnant?' I enquired. 'That's quite a miracle, isn't it?'

'Yes, and we're all so delighted that she looks like bringing it off this time. All right, my darling Digby, run along now, but don't forget.'

*

'Who is poor Mr Pettigrew?' I asked, when we had rattled through the remaining cards and moved on to the kitchen. 'And why does he rate such special treatment?'

Albert was not in evidence and, judging by the state of things, had not sufficiently recovered to resume his duties. There was a mound of unwashed crockery stacked up on the draining-board, including the familiar red thermos.

Betsy emerged from the larder carrying some biscuit tins and a wrapped loaf:

'Gerald Pettigrew? Don't you remember? He's Mamma's solicitor.'

'Oh, him! But I thought he was dead.'

'No, that's the old man. He looked after Mamma's affairs for years but young Gerald took over the senior partnership about six months ago. Well, he's not all that young now, I suppose, but he and I used to see a lot of each other when we were children, and it's always hard to accept that people you've known then grow old, just like everyone else. An ugly old mug he was, too, but such a dear; steadfast and true. He insisted on coming down today, poor old Gerald. I said he wasn't to bother, because we could easily call and see him in his office, but he wouldn't hear of it, even though it must be rather a strain for him. Could you get me some butter out, my honey-bee? I expect there's some in the refrigerator.'

Somewhat mystified, I did as she asked and the flow continued:

'That's mainly why I thought we should lay on something for them to eat when they get back from church. God knows, I don't want to turn it into some sort of grotesque cocktail party, but I usually try to have a little something ready for Gerald when he comes down. After all, it's not as though he could stop off at an hotel for a meal.'

'Why ever not, Betsy? I suppose he's got two legs, hasn't he?'

She gaped at me for a moment, then turned away, laughing.

'No, my duck, I'm afraid that's just what he hasn't got. They were shot to pieces in the war, when he was in the Navy, and he's paralysed from the waist down. Poor Gerald, he's always so plucky and jolly about it. If you only saw him sitting down you'd never guess there was anything wrong, but he has to be carried about like a baby and put in and out of his wheelchair. He has a folding one now, which goes in the boot of his car.'

'Goodness, Betsy, I'm so sorry. I had no idea.'

'Why should you, my lamb? My fault for not mentioning it, but we've all got so used to it that we hardly think of it any more.'

'Does he have someone to look after him?'

'Oh yes, Peter. A dear man. He drives the car and does everything for Gerald, just like a sweet old nannie. The story goes that Gerald saved his life in the war, but I don't know how true it is. Now, do you suppose sand-wiches and wine will be enough, or ought I to try and make something which can be heated up when they get back? Oh dear, I do wish Albert's wife had just had the decency to stay until all this was over. I could go quite mad when I think of her dishing up beautiful meals for that grubby little Ted Williams while we're all in this state. And Albert's such a nice, clean, considerate man. I can't make her out at all.'

'No accounting for the human heart,' I reminded her, thinking of Jasper, as it happened. 'I could knock up a few cheese straws if you like? They're rather my forte.'

'Oh, Tessa, could you really? You are a dear child! And that would give me a chance to get some of this washing-up out of the way. I've tried putting it into the machine, but it doesn't seem to work very well for me. You'll find some flour in the larder and I expect you know how to use the oven, don't you?'

'I'll soon find out,' I assured her, 'but let me come there and wash my hands before I start.'

She had placed the red thermos in the sink, filling it from the hot tap, and she moved it to one side.

'So you've got over your phobias, whatever they were?' I asked her.

'You're a sharp one, aren't you?' she answered placidly.

'Well, people don't normally go staggering around the place and throwing fits because of an old thermos,' I pointed out. 'From which I concluded that this one had disagreeable associations for you.'

'You're quite right, but wasn't I an old silly? Just because poor Mamma had her last drink from it before she died, I had to have all these stupid nightmares. I couldn't rid myself of the idea that the milk might . . . well, you know . . . have gone a bit sour or something, and it had upset her. The slightest physical shock was enough to bring on an attack, you see, which could have been fatal, and for a time I worked myself into a fine old state about it.'

'But you don't any longer believe there was anything wrong with the milk?'

'No, no, I'm positive there wasn't. To be honest, Tessa, I don't think the idea would have got such a hold on me in the first place, if it hadn't been for Jasper. I very foolishly mentioned it to him and he got quite worried about it. That did alarm me, because you know what he's like in the ordinary way? But he actually wanted me to get Dr Macintosh to have the remains of the milk analysed. I agreed to do that, just to put his mind at rest, you know, but then we couldn't find the thermos and that made everything worse than ever; but of course it was all nonsense.'

'But you hadn't drunk any of the milk yourself, presumably?'

'No, but it wouldn't have helped much if I had. I might not have noticed if there'd been anything wrong.'

'Why's that? Have you lost your sense of taste?'

'No, my dove, but I always stir some of my lovely malt mixture into it. Some people can't bear it because it's so sweet, and at the same time rather fishy-tasting, if you know what I mean; but so good and nourishing, specially if one hasn't had time for more than a snack or two during the day. Anyway, it's all over and done with now and we can forget about it. Albert is most meticulous about these things and when I plucked up courage to question him he assured me that he had filled the thermos himself, from an unopened bottle which had gone straight into the fridge that morning.'

'What I don't understand, Betsy, is what the nurse was doing, so that you had to be waiting on Maud at all at that time of night.'

For some reason this sent her into a fluster again:

'What nurse? What are you talking about, Tessa?'

'Jasper told me there was one on duty all night. Not true?'

'Oh, you're becoming as bad as all the rest of them,' she said pettishly. 'Always on at me to leave everything to those nurses, but why should I? They were all right, up to a point; very efficient, I daresay, when it came to medical matters, but they didn't take the same interest. You couldn't expect it; specially Maureen, the night nurse. She was a nice enough little thing in her way, and so pretty; but a bit careless sometimes, you know. Besides, it was a pleasure for me to look after Mamma and take care of those little extra things which a nurse wouldn't bother about.'

'So half the time, I suppose, you sent them off to the pictures and did the work yourself?'

'No, I didn't,' she said firmly. 'I was tempted to, many times, but I wouldn't have dared, when Dr Macintosh might pop in at any hour of the day or night. They'd have got into awful trouble if one of them hadn't been on duty. No, my darling, what happened that last time, the night Mamma died, was that I heard her bell ringing, so I just put my head round the door to make sure everything was all right and there was Maureen fast asleep on her camp-bed on the landing. I didn't stop to wake her and when I discovered it was just that Mamma was feeling thirsty there wasn't any need for it. I'd thought at the time that Albert's wife had put a little too much salt in the consommé for dinner, and I simply went back to my room and fetched her some milk from my thermos. But she only drank a little drop, because she complained that it tasted so horribly bitter. So I went down to the kitchen and heated up some more from a fresh bottle, and sat with her for a little while until she went to sleep. But you see, my dearest, she never properly woke up again. She must have gone into some sort of coma, I suppose.

Perhaps I dozed off too, because all I remember is hearing these terrible gasping noises . . . Then, of course, I ran and got Maureen at once. Luckily she was . . . she was awake by then, but it was too late to do anything. Poor Mamma died before Dr Macintosh could get here and I've been plaguing myself ever since with the idea that there was something wrong with the milk. I hadn't dared utter a word to anyone but Jasper, but you're such a sharp little Tessa, aren't you? And to be honest with you, my dearie, it's quite a relief to bring my silly ghosts out into the daylight. I was overwrought, you know, that's all it was; and now we can both forget every word about it, can't we, my lamb?'

The kitchen door opened before I could give any assurances, false or otherwise, on this point and Piers, Margot's elder son, came in. As usual, he was a fairly breathtaking sight, being tall and elegant, and combining a Michelangelo profile with his mother's beautiful dark eyes; and he and I were no doubt in perfect agreement in considering him to be one of the most handsome young men alive. We might conceivably have differed over his character, however, and furthermore his charm, although rigidly within the authentic Stirling pattern, was somehow forced and self-conscious, often causing those on the receiving end to feel embarrassed rather than exhilarated.

'Teeny crisis, Auntie darling,' he informed Betsy, when the hugging was over, 'Sophie is convinced that the miscarriage is imminent. I don't suppose you have any milk of magnesia, or anything of that kind handy?'

'Oh dear!' she wailed, sounding deeply concerned. 'I don't know, Piers. We may have, but would that really be the best thing for her? Oughtn't we to ask darling Dr

Macintosh to call? He's going to the funeral in any case, so it wouldn't be any trouble for him.'

'Yes, that would be lovely, of course. Sophie would adore it, but in the meantime some magnesia would be a great help in staving the thing off. This is her fourth miscarriage in four months, so one gets to know the form. Perhaps darling Tessa could find some for us, if you're terribly, terribly busy?'

'Yes, would you, Tessa?' Betsy asked me. 'It will be in Mamma's bathroom cupboard, if we have any, and Dr Macintosh's number is on the pad by my bed. Just ask him if he would be very sweet and call in on his way to the Church.'

'And do break the good news to Sophie, my angel,' Piers added. 'It will pep her up enormously to have a real live doctor taking an interest. Oh, but aren't you the good, kind Tessa? Whatever should we do without you, I ask myself.'

I did not wait to hear the answer to this question but nevertheless paused outside the door to catch what followed it and heard Piers say, still in his fulsome, over-pitched voice:

'Oh, by the way, Auntie darling, I hate to bother you when you've got so much on your poor old plate, but there is just one tiny thing.'

'What's that my pet?'

'Such nonsense, really; it couldn't matter less, but I've been looking everywhere in Grandmamma's bedroom and I just can't find those tapes I left for her.'

There was a fractional pause before I heard Betsy say:

'So sorry, my chick, but I'm afraid I can't help you there. I've no idea what became of them. Never mind!

We'll all have a good look round later on and I'm sure we'll be able to find them.'

V

(i)

SOPHIE was reclining on a drawing-room sofa, watched over with tender solicitude by her grandfather-in-law, Dickie Travers, and rather more inscrutably by a black Persian cat curled up at her side. I had often detected a strong feline strain in Sophie's chemistry and I think the cats must have recognised it too, for she was one of the very few human beings whose attentions they would tolerate.

Outwardly, she was a tiny, doll-like creature with exquisite enamelled looks and a thin, metallic voice to match. She and Piers had been married for three years and there had been more than one miscarriage, so far no children. This was one reason that was often given for their marriage so nearly foundering but I think there were others as well.

I went across to her and she opened her pain-filled eyes and stretched out a miniature claw for the glass I was holding. She then took two sips from it and screwed up her face in disgust, which was hardly surprising. Having failed to find magnesia in any shape or form, I had dissolved an aspirin in water and then stirred in a dollop of toothpaste.

Smiling his benign smile, Dickie had risen to greet me. He, too, was a minor work of art in his way; a specimen of authentic or good reproduction Edwardiana, nurtured and polished in a score of drawing-room comedies.

Whether by accident or design, he had been cast during his early career in a succession of rôles portraying the uppermost crust of the English nobility; and so accomplished had he become in them that, whereas the parts had begun by fitting him like a glove, as time went by the glove had become a second skin.

Nor had age diminished this glory for in his middle years he had enraptured audiences even more with his portly, philosophical dukes than with the languid and frivolous variety of his youth. So undisputed was his pre-eminence in this field that the point had come where every fashionable dramatist with his finger on the pulse had got into the way of creating his earls and marquises in the image of Dickie Travers instead of the other way round.

Sadly enough, according to Toby, my invariable, sometimes reliable informant in these matters, it was his very success in this line which had caused his marriage to break up. Being in such constant demand in Shaftesbury Avenue had meant that he was very rarely available to follow the Stirling drum on its regular and triumphant processions round three of the five continents. Maud did not cease to love and adore him but backsliding in this department was one of numerous defects which she would not tolerate in a husband or lover.

Although now in his seventies and long retired, he was still erect and immaculately turned out, with a wholesome pink face and the most pristine of white hair. On this occasion he was wearing a black and white check suit, which could have been delivered from the tailors that very morning, and his handmade shoes had the sheen of chestnuts straight from their green cases. Since he hadn't a thing in the world to do except walk round the corner to his club, sit there for a couple of hours and then walk back again, there was nothing specially admirable in so much elegance, but it was none the less quite a joy to the beholder. Moreover there was a certain gallantry in his unswerving good humour, however foolish, and I knew that no matter how grievously he might feel Maudie's loss, his code would never permit his betraying a hint of self-pity.

'This poor gel's 'avin' a shockin' go of the collywobbles,' he informed me, looking fondly at Sophie and playing his usual leap-frog with the consonants.

Sophie obediently gave a slight shudder and then, to my astonishment and gratification, tossed off the remaining aspirin and toothpaste in one brave gulp.

'Ugh, horrible,' she complained in her tinny voice, 'but whatever it is it seems to be working. I think the pain's going off.'

'That's good,' I said. 'Just lie still and Dr Macintosh will be here quite soon. You must do exactly as he tells you. You may find his approach slightly eccentric, but don't be fooled. In the field of medical science he is pure magic.'

'Clever fellah,' Dickie agreed. 'Most amusin'. Funny thing. Thought he might be related to a fellah I knew at the Garrick. Fellah called Jock Macintosh. Shockin' bounder. But he never even heard of the fellah.'

Sophie did not look particularly reassured by this build-up but with miraculous timing the subject of it entered the room as the last echo died away. Evidently, though, he had forgotten the purpose of his visit and the first five minutes were given over to some fairly searching probes into the state of Dickie's gammy leg. Dr Macintosh then went on to tell us a little about his own ulcer, which was giving him gyp, and followed this up by remarking that he'd been passing the time of day with that extraordinary chap, Pettigrew, whom he'd run into in the hall. However, a moan or two from Sophie eventually brought him round to the subject of an impending miscarriage and Dickie and I left them to hold their consultation in private.

There was no one in the hall but I could hear bellowing booms from the morning-room, where presumably Betsy was entertaining Mr Pettigrew, so I nipped back to the kitchen to get to work on the cheese straws. Robin came in as I was taking them out of the oven and, succumbing to his admiring comments, I allowed him to eat some of the frizzled bits round the edges of the tin.

I then asked him why he had not gone straight to the church, in accordance with schedule, and he replied that he had thought it would be a smart move to park his car in the Rectory drive, so as to make a quick getaway when the time came. He had been unable to place the car in the exact spot of his choosing because there was a little striped, four-wheeled VW beetle, with daisies painted on it, standing just inside the gate.

'That's Digby's contraption,' I said. 'Wouldn't you know?'

'So having got as far as this,' Robin went on, 'I decided to look in and see how you were getting on, and also check up on any murders which may have taken place since we last met.'

'Okay, Robin, but I think that joke's getting a bit frayed now. I admit that I may have magnified things a little, but I still think Betsy is afraid there was something not quite right about Maud's death, even though she has been at such pains to deny it. Well, that's partly why, of course. The lady doth protest a thought too much. All the same, whatever mischief there may have been, it's now quite clear that no one set out to harm Maudie.'

'Well, that's something, at least. How do you know?'

I described the set up with the night nurse, adding: 'So even if Betsy did take rather too much on herself, as Jasper was hinting, it is simply not possible for anyone to have foreseen that Maudie would ring for a drink during the night, that the nurse would have been asleep and not heard her when she did so, and that Betsy wouldn't have drunk any of the milk from her thermos.'

'Very logical thinking, but I take it you have not yet abandoned your lovely idea that the milk had been poisoned, although I suppose you are now working on the assumption that it was intended for Betsy?'

'As to that, I shall keep an open mind,' I told him. 'I still think there may have been something wrong with the milk, and obviously Betsy does, too. Not poison, necessarily, but why shouldn't some well-meaning person have decided to give Betsy a stiff sleeping pill, for instance?'

'For what purpose?'

'Just to calm her down a bit. Because she was getting so fussed.'

'Oh, that's rather a tame solution,' Robin said. He had begun to pace up and down the kitchen in a heavily abstracted manner, running restlesss fingers through his wavy locks, though not neglecting to help himself to a couple of cheese straws as he passed the table.

'I'll tell you what, though, Tessa,' he then announced gravely. 'If there was something wrong about Maud's death, it looks as though Betsy must have been responsible. No one else, as you've pointed out, could have engineered it by remote control, but just consider how simple it would have been for her! She had only to send the nurse on some fictitious errand to the kitchen, then nip in and poison her mother and Bob's your uncle. The story about the thermos could have been sheer fabrication.'

'I've thought of that, naturally,' I said, pretending to take him seriously, 'but I'm afraid it doesn't stand up. In the first place there would have been no occasion to question the timing of Maud's death, if Betsy hadn't raised it herself. Secondly, she had no motive.'

'Oh, I shouldn't let that bother you,' he said cheerfully. 'Just keep digging away and you'll turn one up in the end.'

By an odd coincidence I was to find a first-class, gold-plated one only a few hours later, and with no digging at all.

(ii)

Margot came downstairs wearing a black fur pancake, which looked as though it might originally have belonged to a guardsman and subsequently been remodelled for Davy Crockett. Presumably it was her special funeral hat, for it was unseasonable in a heatwave as well as unbecoming. Nevertheless she succeeded as usual in conveying a marked impression of delicate breeding in her particular brand of dowdiness.

'Are you going to walk down to the church with me?' she enquired, eyeing my flour-spattered dress with some disdain. 'That will be delightful, but you need a wash and brush up first, don't you?'

'No, I'm staying here,' I replied. 'Betsy can't face it and I've promised to sit it out with her.'

It cost quite an effort to say this, for although I did not find her congenial or sympathetic, Margot had perfected the art of inducing others to take her at her own valuation, which was about as high as you could go. She was so sublimely complacent that one felt almost flattered to be put in one's place by her and to disobey her commands bordered on downright ingratitude.

'How tiresome of her! I cannot think why she has to make such a fuss.'

'Robin's going,' I said defensively. 'He's just left. And I suppose you'll have Dickie and the boys to support you?'

'Evidently not, my dear. Piers thinks he ought to stay with Sophie until the last minute. She's lying down in Betsy's room now and feeling very sorry for herself, I gather. As for Digby, I've simply no idea where he's got to. You haven't seen him, I suppose?'

'Not lately. I thought he was with you.'

She did not deign to comment on this, but seeing Dickie come into the hall turned her attention to him.

'Oh, there you are, Father! You and I seem to be the only pair with our wits about us this morning. Really, what a madhouse! Shall we go along now?'

'Ready when you are, old gel. Just get me titfer.'

I watched them set off together down the drive, two stately, upright figures, both firmly entrenched in their separate rôles, neither of which permitted the faintest whiff of spontaneous emotion breaking through the surface. There was something quite confidence-inspiring in the sight of them and yet, when they reached the gate, I had a nagging feeling that there was something missing from the picture. It was not until I had turned indoors again that I realised what this was, and went out to verify it. Robin's car was parked away to my left, twenty yards or so inside the drive. Between it and the gate there was an empty space, signifying that the daisy-covered beetle had been driven away.

Gerald Pettigrew, had left some minutes before and I found Betsy alone in the morning-room. She looked chilled and wretched and appeared to have aged several years in the last half hour. Evidently, her grief went much deeper than I had realised and, whatever Robin might say, I was convinced that this time, at any rate, her distress was genuine. Uncertain how to treat the situation, I said nothing and seated myself in the armchair facing hers.

She looked up and smiled bleakly at me once, but for the most part simply stared down into the fireplace, rumpling the great big sensible handkerchief between her hands.

After ten minutes the silence was making me nervous and I suggested it might be a good plan to give ourselves a job of work, such as laying out some plates in the dining-room.

'Not just yet, my duck. I'd rather sit here quietly and think a few things out. Albert can probably cope with all that. He's feeling a bit better now, but he preferred not to go to the church. I believe he means to visit the grave on his own; later on, when everyone has gone. He's a Catholic, you know, so I suppose our services don't have quite the same meaning for him.'

She reeled all this off in a flat, toneless way, which worried me even more than the former silence, and I said: 'Should I get you a drink then, Betsy?'

'What? A drink? Oh no, thank you, my pet. I had one with Gerald, just to keep him company. He wants to talk to us all when the others get back. Did I tell you that? He wants us all to hear about Mamma's will and so on . . .'

Her voice trailed away to desolate mumble and, assuming my briskest manner, I said:

'Another ordeal for you, poor Betsy, but I expect it's sensible to do everything according to the ritual. It's always easier to get through these bad times when everyone has a script to follow. All the same, he won't want Robin and me, so we'll fade out as soon as the others return.'

'Oh no, you mustn't do that,' she wailed, looking more distraught than ever. 'No, please stay, my love. I couldn't face it on my own. Besides, Mamma was very fond of you, you know.'

I could not see what this had to do with it, but she was too absorbed in her own miseries to listen to argument; so I threw out a few clichés about how fond I'd been of Maudie and how much better it was for her not to have lived on in pain, etcetera, and promised to stay at least until we had consulted Robin about it.

She seemed to take this as outright consent and smiled at me more peaceably. 'That's right, my honey-bun; such a comfort you are!'

Gerald Pettigrew, with the faithful Peter in tow, was the first to return, since he had been unable to get his wheelchair down to the graveside, and at the sound of his voice booming out in the hall Betsy livened up a bit and flapped around offering him food and drink. She was all for pushing him straight off to the dining-room, but he flung out his arm like a driver signalling a right turn, saying that Pete could bring him a nosh and a bottle of the best plonk in the drawing-room as he had some papers to sort out before the balloon went up and considered it advisable to get the business out of the way with all speed, and then get cracking back to London. He explained that he and some of the lads had had one hell of a thrash the night before and such rumpuses were apt to leave him feeling a bit frail these days.

He was covered from the waist down by a thick tartan rug, but his upper half looked far from frail for he had a bullish neck, a round, jovial face with sticking out ears and innocent-looking blue eyes. It was the kind of head and shoulders one would have expected to see on the rugger field, rather than being dragged through life in an invalid chair, and I did not doubt that Betsy's assessment was correct and that so great were his will and courage that his disability was the last pretext he would have used to procure special treatment.

As she obediently turned the chair in the direction of the drawing-room, he looked back over his shoulder and called out that he would be pleased to see me, along with all the other bods, when they foregathered later on; and that tow-headed husband of mine as well if he could spare the time. Since Betsy, in her flurry or forgetfulness, had omitted to introduce us, I was rather impressed to discover that he not only knew exactly who I was but exactly who Robin was too. On the principle that it is a mistake to underrate anyone, I cautioned myself not to be taken in by the jolly Jack Tar façade.

Margot and Dickie were the next to arrive, with Digby hot on their heels. In the act of removing her ghastly hat, Margot stared at him with icy disfavour.

'And where have you been, pray?'

'Well, you know . . . same place as everyone else,' he mumbled.

'I didn't see you.'

'No, well, I was at the back . . . you know.'

'No, I do not know. What were you doing at the back? Why weren't you sitting with me?'

'Sorry, Mum, but I got in a bit late. Anyway, I saw you. You were . . . you know . . . in the front pew with Piers and Grandpapa.'

It was a pretty safe guess, as Margot probably realised, for she said no more and went on with the job of disentangling the hat. Moving towards the open front door, I met Robin coming in and we stood there talking for a while.

'How was it?' I asked.

'As you'd expect. Rather grim.'

'You didn't happen to notice Digby?'

'Not that I remember. Why?'

'He's fairly distinctive; I just thought you might have. He's supposed to have been sitting at the back.'

'Really, Tessa, what are you on about now? There was a chap in a wheelchair I noticed, and one or two other oddments of people at the back. I concluded they were local reporters or something, but Digby could have been among them. Does it matter?'

'No, just curiosity. His car's back, anyway. Do you want a drink?'

'No thanks. Strictly speaking, I should be on my way. How about you?'

'I'd leave too, if I could, but it's a bit complicated. You see . . .'

Betsy emerged from the dining-room carrying a tray of sandwiches and wine. She laid a hand on Robin's arm, causing the tray to wobble, so I took it from her.

'Come along, Robin dearie,' she said, 'Gerald particularly wants you to stay and hear what he has to tell us and I'd be so very grateful if you would. Tessa, darling, since you've got the tray, could you just run up and give it to Sophie for me? She's lying down in my room. I'd ask Piers but he's being such a help to me in the dining-room. I'm afraid I'd forgotten all about Sophie and she may be feeling peckish, poor lamb.'

*

Maud's bedroom was at the head of the staircase on the first landing, with her bathroom on the left of it, and I remembered that Betsy's room was two doors down on the right, separated from her mother's by a second, more austere bathroom. The door was ajar and, pushing it further open with my knee, I saw the poor lamb curled up and fast asleep on the bed, wrapped in Betsy's old Jaeger dressing-gown. I set the tray down on the bedside table but she did not stir and I decided not to wake her.

The wardrobe door was also open, swinging a little on its hinges, and passing it on my way out I automatically pushed it to. There must have been something wrong with the catch, though, for it immediately flew open again, wider than before and hitting a chair leg in the process. I glanced over at the bed but there was still no movement, so I left her to it and crept out of the room.

'Just as well, poppet,' Betsy said, when I handed in my report. 'Gerald won't mind whether she's there or not, and Piers can tell her about it afterwards. Personally, my darling, I'm rather relieved.'

I did not ask her why this was, but followed her into the drawing-room, where the audience was now beginning to assemble.

VI

ISOLATED in his shell of boredom and impatience, Robin occupied a sofa as far removed as he could place himself from Margot and Piers, who stood together by the fireplace chatting as unconcernedly as though they were at a cocktail party. However, this had small significance because when it came to putting on an act they had both been trained in a hard school. Less versed in the art, Jasper was strutting about the room, continually shaking back his romantic lock of hair and nervously nibbling at a sandwich.

'What are you doing here?' he asked me rudely.

'Now, my dearest, you mustn't be cross with poor little Tessa. She's been such a help to me.'

'I shall be cross with whoever I please,' he replied, shaking her hand from his arm. 'This is the most grotesque charade I've ever been asked to take part in. I didn't realise that even your family was capable of organising such a farce.'

I sat down beside Robin and Betsy went over to speak to Gerald. A sofa table in the centre of one wall, between the two windows, had been pulled forward to make an improvised desk for him. Seated behind it, with only his top half visible, there was nothing to show that he was in any way abnormal and it may have been the confidence which this knowledge inspired which had toned down his exuberant manner. He sat quietly sifting through his papers, as though oblivious to the rest of us, although he did look up and smile as Betsy approached. They exchanged a few words and then she turned round and called out to Margot:

'Gerald is ready to begin now. Do you know where Dickie and Digby have got to?'

'I have sent Digby to fetch Albert,' Margot replied.

'That was quite unnecessary,' Gerald told her. 'And what have you done with your father?'

'I believe he has gone for a stroll in the garden,' she said primly.

'I was always on at Mamma to have one installed downstairs,' Betsy confessed, joining Robin and me on the sofa, and she sighed deeply, as though regretting that vindication had come too late.

Dickie entered the room at this point and stood just inside the door, gazing amiably around and beaming benevolently at all of us.

''Allo, 'allo, 'allo! Board meetin' started already?'

'No, dear,' Betsy assured him. 'We shouldn't dream of starting without you. Have you seen Digby by any chance?'

'Funny thing. I saw him boltin' upstairs. "What's the fellah up to now?" I thought. Go and get him down, shall I?'

Not waiting for consent, he turned and ambled out of the room again. Whereupon Jasper flung himself down in an armchair uttering a loud groan, Margot raised her eyebrows and Betsy murmured that it really was too bad of them, when Gerald had gone to all this trouble and must be feeling quite whacked.

Dickie reappeared a few minutes later, accompanied by Digby, looking flustered and apprehensive.

'I'm frightfully sorry,' he said, addressing his mother, 'but I can't find him. I've looked everywhere . . . you know . . . in their flat and everything, but he's not there.'

'Which is just as well,' Gerald announced, 'because if you had I should have been compelled to send him away again. What I have to tell you is unofficial and strictly for your ears alone. So, if you've all now finished popping in and out, I may as well begin.'

After the inevitable round of coughing and fidgeting which follows such preludes, there was silence and he went on:

'You'll be getting letters and copies of the will from my office in due course, but there are certain aspects which can't be dealt with in correspondence; so, in order to spare everyone as much confusion as possible, and also to avoid future recriminations, I've asked you to be good enough to spare me ten minutes of your time now. Right?'

He looked round at each face in turn and there was no flippancy or impatience to be detected on them now. The general reaction, which I shared, was one of slightly uneasy curiosity.

'As most of you know,' Gerald continued, 'Maud made minor alterations and codicils to her will on several occasions during the last months of her life. This is not a particularly rare phenomenon with elderly people during a terminal illness. It sometimes stems from forgetfulness and failing mental powers, and sometimes from sheer self-preservation. The threat of cutting some relative or companion out of a will can be quite an effective whip for bringing that person to heel. However, I cannot emphasise too strongly that neither of these conditions applied to Maud. She was in full possession of her faculties, remarkably so for her age, right up to the day of her death, as I happen to know at first hand. I beg your pardon?'

He had been interrupted by a loud squawk from Jasper.

'Did you say something?' Gerald enquired.

'Not exactly,' Jasper replied in an amused voice. 'What you heard was merely a comment on your claim to know any such thing at first hand. I apologise if it put you off your stroke, but since it can't possibly be true . . .'

'You are wrong, as it happens, Craig, but I'll come back to the point in a minute. To return to what I was saying: Maud was in no sense senile and nor, to the best of my knowledge, did she ever threaten or attempt to influence anyone by disclosing or hinting at the terms of her will. All my recent consultations with her on this subject were conducted in the privacy of her bedroom, and she refused categorically to instruct me either by letter or telephone. As you know, I visited her several times during this spring and summer. It was not always strictly convenient to do so,' he added wryly, 'but Maud was adamant and I do not have to tell any of you that she was not a person whose demands were easy to resist. What you are evidently not all aware of is that my last visit occurred within a few hours of her death.'

It was plain from the stir which went round the room that Jasper had not been alone in his ignorance of this fact, although Betsy betrayed no surprise continuing, as before, to make pleated patterns with her handkerchief as though her life depended on it. Margot was the one to voice the general incredulity and, as usual, she managed to sound faintly insulting.

'I'm afraid you must be mistaken, Gerald. We were all here on that day, the whole family; though, God knows, none of us guessed it would be the last time we should see her. But I certainly don't recall hearing anything about a visit from you.'

'I may have misled you by calling it a few hours. To be precise, I was with her from eleven until noon. She invited me to stay for lunch, but, contrary to her cherished beliefs, I had other clients besides herself and I preferred to drive back to London. Pete remembers the occasion well and so, I believe, does Betsy?'

Without raising her eyes and speaking exclusively to the handkerchief, Betsy mumbled: 'Gerald is quite right. I am sorry I forgot to tell you, but I was out at my meeting when he came; and then you all arrived and Mamma was so pleased and excited and everything. It must have gone out of my head. Besides, as Gerald says, she was always sending for him and there was no reason to suppose that this time was any more important than the others. Do forgive me, though.'

'It wouldn't have made the slightest difference if you had told them,' Gerald said coolly. 'I have raised the point for one purpose only.'

He paused to take in another brief survey of his audience before continuing:

'It was simply to impress upon you that it would be useless, as well as undignified, to contest this will, either now or in the future. It was drawn up according to her explicit instructions and signed and witnessed in my presence. I am satisfied that she was in her right mind and understood what she was doing, and I would be prepared to repeat this on oath.'

This ominous statement provoked a general spluttering and muttering of alarm or displeasure, but once again Margot was the only one to complain aloud.

'Really, Gerald, I can't imagine why you find it necessary to bully us. Surely your job is to tell us about Mamma's will and keep your comments to yourself? I daresay you're getting a great deal of fun out of lecturing us all but if it's leading up to some rubbish about Mamma leaving everything to a cat's home, kindly say so and have done with it. We're perfectly capable of making up our own minds about what steps to take.'

'I say, hold on, ol' gel,' Dickie waffled in a faintly uneasy way. 'No point in gettin' the wind up till we hear what the fellah has to say.'

'That is exactly my point,' Margot told him angrily. 'If he can be persuaded to tell us what that is.'

Gerald had flushed so violently that the sun shining through the window at his back made his ears look literally on fire. He glanced enquiringly at Betsy and she nodded, saying in a braver tone:

'It's all right, Gerald dear, you mustn't mind what we say. We're all a bit on edge today.'

'Speak for yourself,' Margot said sharply, and Digby reached out and grasped her hand. She shook him off, disregarding his imploring look.

Gerald took only a second or two to regain his self-possession and then continued as though there had been no interruption.

'Having made my own position clear, I shall now outline the main clauses of this, the last will and testament of Maud Stirling, revoking all former wills and signed by her in my presence and in the presence of Maureen Bilson, S.R.N., of 21, Cross Street, Dulwich, S.E., and of Mrs Olive Chalmers, Masseuse and Physiotherapist, of 2, Mayfield Drive, Storhampton-on-Thames. They are relatively brief and I should be obliged if you could all remain silent until I have finished. I propose to give you the terms in layman's language, more or less as dictated to me by Maud, and omitting most of the legal trimmings which might be puzzling to you. One: To my faithful friend and servant, Albert Matthieu, I leave a capital sum, the exact amount to be fixed upon later, to be invested in an annuity which shall provide him with an income for life of two thousand pounds per annum, free of tax.'

When these words dropped among his listeners an audible sigh passed round the room and normal breathing processes went into action again. The bequest may have been a little more generous than I, for one, had anticipated, but the substance of it was no doubt the kind of thing they had all been expecting before the session began. Everything, one felt, was after all turning out according to plan.

Seemingly unaware of the slackening of tension, Gerald continued:

'There follows a short list of minor bequests, which again I shall give you in the terms they were presented to me: To my grandson, Piers Roche, my diaries, letters, photographs and all other records of my public life still extant, to make what use of them he chooses and I also appoint the said Piers Roche my official biographer. To my grandson, Digby Roche, I bequeath whichever one of my motor cars he may prefer, together with a sufficient sum of money to cover the road tax and insurance for a period of one year from the date of my death.'

Neither grandson looked particularly ecstatic about these windfalls, but Margot, now exuding good humour, beamed at both of them with great complacency, and the reading continued:

'To my former husband, Richard Travers, the sum of five thousand pounds and my collection of Fabergé ornaments, which he has so often admired. To my friend, Theresa Price, my ruby and diamond ring, inscribed on the back with my initials, in recognition of the many hours of her company which she so generously gave.'

Betsy had pushed the handkerchief at me even before the tears had started to my eyes, but I blinked them back into reserve for a later occasion, for Gerald was still intoning in the same dispassionate voice:

'To my daughter, Marguerite Roche, my sable coat and the portrait of myself by Augustus John, which I trust she will see fit to hang in a prominent place, wherever she may happen to be living.'

There followed a deathly silence, in which nobody had the courage to look at Margot. Dickie half rose in his chair, then lost his nerve and subsided again.

'Go on,' Margot said between clenched teeth.

'There is not much to add,' Gerald informed her. 'One remaining clause, as follows: To my daughter, Elisabeth Craig, the residue of my estate, including all my property, financial holdings, personal effects and goods and chattels, absolutely and unconditionally, to use and dispose of as she wishes.'

Still speaking and with no change of tone, Gerald folded his papers together.

'That's the lot. Betsy and I are joint executors and, to forestall the inevitable questions, I am able to tell you, through long and intimate acquaintance with the subject, that the estate is likely to come out in probate at something between one-quarter and one-third of a million.'

For a moment I feared that Margot had been afflicted by a mild stroke and was about to crash to the ground in a stupor, but her voice remained stonily controlled as she said:

'What utter balderdash! I don't believe a word of it.'

'I am sorry to hear that,' Gerald told her, 'although it is more or less what I expected. You have my sympathy, but there is nothing in the world that I or anyone else can do about it. You are naturally free to take advice elsewhere, but I have already warned you what the outcome would be.'

'You have indeed,' she replied, 'and one does begin to glimpse the motive behind all that pompous preamble.'

Gerald had stretched out his hand to a bell, which had been placed just within reach and his fingers closed tightly round the handle.

'What are you implying, Margot?'

'It's obvious enough, surely? You had the best of reasons for warning us off. The less we enquired into this farcical document the better it would be for you. I don't know what your reasons may have been, or what devices you used to trick Mamma into signing it, but if you think you can coerce me into believing that this so-called will expressed her true intentions, you are very sadly mistaken.'

'Oops, now! Take it easy, old gel,' Dickie protested, getting right out of his chair this time.

'I suppose you understand what you have just accused me of?' Gerald enquired. 'Fraudulence of a kind which would not only get me barred from practising for the rest of my life, but would also carry serious criminal charges. I would remind you that there were half a dozen witnesses to your allegations, two of whom are unconnected with your family.'

Margot glanced contemptuously at Robin and me, as though registering our presence for the first time.

'Is that why you insisted on their being here? Are you threatening me, Gerald?'

'No, I think it is you who are threatening me, or attempting to. I am simply advising you to say no more until you have had time to reflect on your position, and if necessary to take legal advice.'

He then shook the bell and Pete's head instantly popped round the door.

'Ready to move off, mate?' he asked.

'Yes, please. You can take me to the car now.'

Pete advanced into the room and pulled the sofa table sideways, so that Gerald could manoeuvre the wheelchair from behind it.

'I'd like to see you in my office as soon as possible, Betsy,' he said, as he swivelled himself round. 'Monday, if you can. Ring my secretary first thing and make an appointment, will you?'

Pete held the door wide for him and we watched in silence as he rolled himself through it and out of sight.

Robin and I followed a few seconds later, he having dragged me out of the room practically by the hair.

'I'm sure we shouldn't leave Betsy alone with the howling wolves,' I protested. 'I had a strong impression that Margot was about to tell the boys to lynch her.'

'She'll be all right. She's got Jasper to protect her and it would be much better for them to get the first round of recriminations over in private. Less embarrassing all round.'

'But the stupid thing is, Robin, that it's all so unnecessary. Margot has only to command Betsy to hand over half the loot and she'd oblige without a murmur, with a pound of emeralds thrown in.'

'Maybe, but it wouldn't be quite the same, would it? Specially for a proud old thoroughbred like Margot. All very fine to inherit a quarter of a million; not quite such fun to have it doled out as charity by the dowdy old sister you'd spent the best part of your life openly despising. Besides, she would have to reckon with Jasper. He might not be quite so keen on going shares.'

'Oh, Jasper doesn't . . .' I began, then lost the thread as my attention became diverted to another quarter. The front door was still open to the warm afternoon and from the corner of my eye I had glimpsed Gerald's car turning in the drive, before beginning its slow, smooth progress to the gate. Halfway there it halted and Pete got out and walked back towards us.

'Message for you from the boss,' he told me. 'Any time you got nothing better to do, he'd like you to give him a buzz at the office. You'll find it in the book under Pettigrew and Barrett. Ask for Mr Gerald. Right?'

'Oh sure. What for, though?'

'No idea, lady. My instructions were to pass on the message.'

'Well, thanks.'

'And what's that all about, do you suppose?' I asked Robin when Pete had marched off again.

'Perhaps he wants to hand over your ring in person. That was a nice thought on Maudie's part, wasn't it?'

'It was her absolute favourite lucky ring,' I said, toying with the idea that this might be the moment for some of the unshed tears to start rolling, but Robin was off on a new tack.

'Listen, Tess, will you be all right on your own now? I've rather outstayed my allotted span as it is.'

'Must you go back to Dedley, then?'

'Yes, I ought to check up on any fresh developments and so forth. My voices tell me that all is not quite such plain sailing there as I could wish. Still, I may be wrong, and if so I'll only need to look in for ten minutes. See you at Toby's this evening. I might even manage to spend the night there, if he can have me.'

'You bet he can. Oh, that would be lovely.'

'Goodbye and soyez de bon courage, then,' he said, using a valediction he had picked up on a visit to Paris the previous year and clung to with great affection ever since.

'I'm afraid I'll need to,' I said, though a good deal more lightheartedly than if I had known how true it was.

VII

(i)

LEFT on my own and uncertain what to do next, I dithered outside the drawing-room for a while, but the sound of acrimonious voices did not tempt me to go in and I sidestepped to the dining-room.

As I had half expected, nothing had been cleared away and there were dirty plates and glasses littered all over the room. I stacked some of them up and went to the pantry to fetch a tray. It was while hunting around for one that I heard a sound from the kitchen and, moving to one side, saw Albert entering by the back door. He was wearing a rakish green hat, which I surmised had once been Dickie's property, and was carrying an elaborate arrangement of roses and carnations which, after a fractional hesitation, he bundled furtively inside the refrigerator of all places. He looked ghastly and, concluding that grief had unhinged him, I ambled forward saying,

'Oh, hallo, Albert. I'm just having a whip round the dining-room. Hope your union won't raise hell,' in the hope of cheering him up with a little light banter.

The response was not enthusiastic. He stared at me, glassy-eyed and blotchy-faced and he swayed a little on his feet as he spoke.

'There is no need to trouble yourself, madam. I shall attend to everything. I had Miss Betsy's permission to go out for a while.'

'That's okay, I was only trying to help.'

Unbending in more senses than one, he flopped into a chair and said in less frigid tones.

'I wished to go down and say my farewell when everyone had gone. I had some little flowers.'

'You mean the ones you just dumped in the refrigerator?'

He got up again and, moving very slowly, placed the hat in a cupboard, took out his white jacket and put it on.

'Yes, they are in the refrigerator. Miss Betsy has told me that it was only for the family to send flowers but that in my case it would be permitted also, because I have been here so many years and Miss Stirling looked upon me as part of the family. I chose these flowers specially. They were her favourites.'

'But you didn't put them on her grave?'

'When I came there it was not as I had expected. So many flowers. Dozens must have sent them. I saw that my offering would be lost among all these, so I say to myself: "Well, I shall wait. In two days, four maybe, these others will be dead and there will be room for mine."'

'So you've put them in cold storage until your moment comes? How very practical!' I said admiringly. 'Will it work?'

'I can try,' he replied. 'We used to do this sometimes with Miss Stirling's orchids when she had too many.'

Betsy came into the kitchen looking fairly distraught, though not, as it happened, in quite such straits as Albert who took another turn for the worse at the sight of her and, in attempting to rise, reeled up against the stove. She was concentrating on me, however, and did not appear to notice.

'Oh, you're still here, Tessa? I thought I heard your voice. Thank goodness for that! Come along and give me a hand in the dining-room, will you? And be a dear boy, Albert, and take some tea to the drawing-room. Nothing to eat, you know; just some cups on a tray.'

'Do I congratulate you?' I asked, when we had moved out of earshot. 'I suppose not, in the circumstances?'

'Oh, don't joke about it, my lamb. You must know it was the very last thing I wanted for Margot, it's been the most wretched shock for her. I've told her over and over again that I mean to share everything with her, but in our hearts we both know that's not the point.'

'I should think it might be some compensation.'

'No, no, no. It's not the money she minds about, you must understand that. It's the hurtfulness of it. Like a slap in the face. I know I should feel just the same, if it were me. Do you think these sandwiches are worth keeping?'

'Perhaps not. Didn't Maud give you an inkling of what she meant to do?'

'Never. Not for one instant. My goodness, if only she had! Don't you realise I'd have done everything in my power to prevent her?'

'Yes,' I agreed. 'I really believe you would.'

'I mean, whoever would have dreamt of such a thing? Mamma adored Margot. Really, one begins to wonder if she's right, and Gerald has made some hideous mistake.'

'He didn't strike me as a man who would make mistakes on that scale.'

'No,' she admitted with a sigh. 'I don't think so either; and he's not crooked. That I refuse to believe. Oh well, we shall get over it and put everything to rights in the end, I daresay. There's still quite a lot of wine left in this bottle, my duck. Perhaps Albert can finish it up.'

'I think he might have had quite a drop already,' I told her.

'Oh, my beloved child, what dreadful things you say sometimes. Poor Albert! He has such a lot to bear at the moment.'

'Talking of that, Betsy, has our mother-to-be surfaced yet?'

'No, but Piers went up to see her about ten minutes ago. He said she was still sound asleep. At least, I think that's what he said. To tell you the truth, I was too worried about Margot to pay proper attention. But you're quite right, my dearie, we really are neglecting her. I expect kind old Dr Macintosh gave her a good, strong sedative, but it must wear off some time. Let's go and see if she's ready for a cup of tea, shall we?'

Evidently she was right about the sedative wearing off because the bedroom was empty, but the first thing that struck me was that the wardrobe door was swinging open again.

'You ought to get something done about that,' I said, once more slamming it shut. 'Probably something wrong with the catch.'

She came up behind me, peering over my shoulder, then said sharply: 'What have you done with the key?'

'Nothing. It's not here.'

'Oh no, of course not. What a fool I am! I put it in my pocket. But, Tessa, it can't have come open by itself. I locked it and took the key out. I'm absolutely certain I did.' Her voice had grown harsh and scared, as though all the dithering sweetness had suddenly been shocked out of her and, rather as though I were some tiresome, inquisitive child, she pushed me aside in order to examine the keyhole for herself.

'It's been forced,' she said in a voice of doom, and I jumped back to avoid a head on collision with the door, as she jerked it wide open and thrust her head inside.

'What on earth for, Betsy? What do you keep in there?'

'Oh, nothing much, my pet,' she replied with some return to her normal manner, and sounding puzzled now, rather than angry. 'Most of my belongings are over at the Stables.'

'Then why should anyone?'

'Never mind, never mind. It has no importance at all, none whatever. The important thing is Sophie. Where can she have got to?'

'Bathroom, probably.'

'Oh dear, do you think so? Perhaps we ought to go and see. She might have fainted.'

'I'll go, Betsy. You have another look through your wardrobe and make sure nothing is missing.'

Sophie was not in either of the bathrooms, although the electric fire over the bath was switched on in one of them, and when I returned to Betsy's room I found that she had vanished as well. I was about to shrug the whole thing off as another of life's minor mysteries when she came staggering in through the French windows from the balcony.

'Oh God! My God! Go and ring up Dr Macintosh. Now, at once. Go on, Tessa. For God's sake, do as I say. Something terrible has happened. There's been a dreadful accident.'

'Sophie?'

'I think so. She must have leaned over the rail and it collapsed. It's all broken anyway, and there's someone lying down there on the terrace. I'm terribly afraid it's her. Oh God, Tessa, could you come with me, after all, and make sure? I don't think I can face it on my own. We could ring the doctor when we know for certain and I have a ghastly feeling that a few more minutes isn't going to make much difference.'

'Come on, then,' I said, running out of the room and downstairs to the morning-room. 'It may not be as bad as you think. Perhaps she's just concussed or something.'

It was far worse than that, however, as I could tell even before I had stepped out on to the terrace. She lay there lifeless as a bundle of washing, one limp arm stretched out and her head lolling. She was still partly covered by the old Jaeger dressing-gown but nothing could disguise the fact that her neck was broken and, for one confused moment, I imagined there was also a dead animal lying beside her. Then I saw that it was Margot's hat, which had been dropped on the terrace.

Automatically I looked up at the balcony and saw that Betsy had been right. The middle section sagged forward; one of the posts which supported it had come clean away from its moorings and was only saved from falling by the fact that it was cushioned in a tangle of broken and twisted vines.

I turned to Betsy, intending to warn her not to stand directly underneath it, and saw that she had picked up the hat and was in the act of throwing it through the morning-room window. I had a feeling that she ought not to do this, but before I could speak she grabbed my arm, grey in the face and trembling from head to foot.

'Dr Macintosh,' she whimpered, pushing me towards the house. 'Don't worry about me, go and get him. Be quick, Tessa, I beg you.'

I did as she asked despite a strong conviction, as I dialled the number, that it should have been the police I was calling.

(ii)

Another half hour went by before the police came, mainly because Betsy insisted on waiting for Dr Macintosh's verdict before making another move. I think she half believed that he had only to pour some magic potion down Sophie's throat to bring her back to life, but when he arrived he carried out only the most cursory examination, before turning indoors again, as I had guessed he would, to telephone the local C.I.D.

In the meantime I had prevailed upon Betsy to call Piers out and break the news to him and he stood with us on the terrace, his head turned away from Sophie and raised up slightly, as though posing for a photograph. His expression on first seeing his wife's body had been compassionate and puzzled rather than grief stricken and he had not uttered a word, or, even more remarkable in a member of that family, shed a tear.

'Which of you found her?' Dr Macintosh demanded, emerging from the house again.

'It was me really,' Betsy said. 'Tessa had gone to look for her in the bathroom, but it occurred to me that she might have gone out to the balcony for some fresh air. That's how I saw the railing had collapsed. So naturally I looked over, as far as I dared you know, and I saw something . . . someone . . . lying there. I guessed at once what had happened. I recognised the dressing-gown, you see.'

'Ah yes, yours, isn't it? Thought I'd seen it somewhere before.'

'She put it on,' Piers explained in a remote voice, 'when I went up to see her. After you'd given her the sedative. She said she felt shivery, so I gave her Betsy's dressing-gown.

'Where was it?' I asked, sidetracked by another memory.

'Where was what?' Piers enquired coldly.

'The dressing-gown. On the bed, or hanging up in the wardrobe, or what?'

'I haven't the faintest idea, my darling. My mind's a complete blank on the subject. Is it important to you?'

'No of course it isn't,' Betsy said, gripping my wrist and digging her finger nails into the skin. 'Tessa's upset, just like the rest of us. She doesn't know what she's saying, poor duck.'

'Well, you'd both better run along indoors now,' said Dr Macintosh, who had been eyeing us all with rather lively curiosity for the past few minutes. 'Piers and I will stop here until the police come. Where's your mother, by the way, Piers?'

'Indoors. Grandpapa and Digby are with her. They're trying to persuade her to go back to London, but I don't think she wants to.'

'She's quite right,' we heard Dr Macintosh say. 'There can be no question of anyone leaving until the police say so.'

'Why do you suppose that is?' Betsy asked me in a troubled voice.

'Oh, it's quite normal,' I assured her. 'They have to establish cause of death and so on; and naturally that involves talking to everyone who might know something about it.'

'But it was an accident. Anybody could see that. It was just very, very unfortunate that no one had thought to warn Sophie about those railings being so rotten. Margot couldn't possibly know anything and I shall tell them so.'

I could see she meant it, too, and I wondered for the very first time whether her protectiveness towards the family and her mania for covering up unpleasantness went slightly beyond the bounds of sanity.

'The point is,' I said, 'and it's something that neither you nor anyone else can prevent, that the police will give Margot a much rougher time if she scoots back to London than if she waits here and answers their questions like a good girl.'

She may have taken it in, or Margot may have seen it for herself, for she was still on the premises when the police bundled in a few minutes later.

Their team was led by Chief Inspector Mackenzie, a stocky, thick-set man, with piggy eyes and a chip on the shoulder which would have been visible from miles away. Having despatched his men and equipment to various parts of the house and grounds, he ordered Betsy to wait in the hall and then herded the rest of us, including Albert, into the drawing-room. Betsy was required to stay behind to show him another room on the ground floor where he could interview each of us in turn.

Calculating that I could easily be placed at the bottom of this list, I asked leave to make a telephone call. He may have imagined that I had lost my head and wished to call my solicitor for he positively glinted with pleasure in telling me that it would be out of the question, since the line must be kept open for police business. Never squeamish about pulling whatever strings came to hand in this tough old world, I murmured that I had merely wished to let my husband know that I should be late home, laying faint stress on his name and rank. On the whole this proved more effective and far less bother than a telephone call because, notwithstanding a glance of purest hatred, I was the first to be summoned to the dining-room when he had set up shop.

Before this happened we were rejoined by Betsy, accompanied by a young, red-faced constable, who closed the door and planted himself in front of it, looking supremely self-conscious.

'What's that man doing here?' Margot demanded in haughty tones.

'Hush, my pet, he's only obeying orders. But I expect you're allowed to sit down, aren't you, officer? Albert, be a dear and bring up a chair for him, will you?'

'But I want to know what he's doing here,' Margot insisted. 'We don't have to be guarded, do we?'

'He is here to prevent our cooking up a story together before we are questioned,' I explained. 'And also to stop us comparing notes afterwards.'

'How dare you talk such nonsense?' Margot stormed, rounding on me in a fury. 'Cooking up a story, indeed! I never heard anything so vulgar in my life. And if you're hinting what I think you are you ought to be ashamed of yourself. I should have thought we had enough to suffer without disgusting innuendos of that kind.'

She was greeted by the usual cries of 'Now, Mother!', 'Hush, Margot!' from all points of the compass, but she refused to be pacified.

'No, I will not be quiet. I consider that Tessa has made a dangerous and malicious statement and I insist that she withdraws it and apologises. I suppose the police have to go blundering around, upsetting everyone, but each of us here knows perfectly well it was an accident. To suggest that anyone meant to harm poor little Sophie is utterly monstrous.'

There I agreed with her, but before I could say so the constable intervened. He had been studiously gazing at his watch during Margot's outburst, the better no doubt to drink in every word, and he now looked over and nodded his head at me:

'The chief inspector is ready to see you now, madam, if you would just step into the dining-room.'

'Now remember what I've said, Tessa,' Margot warned me. 'Just say it was an accident and leave it at that. I hope we can count on your loyalty to that extent.'

She was clearly oblivious of the fact that in issuing these instructions she had fallen slap into the pitfall whose existence she had so vehemently denied but, considering it imprudent to point this out, I went on my way to the dining-room.

No direct reference was made to my illustrious husband and I agreed with the chief inspector that I was Mrs Theresa Price, also known professionally as Theresa Crichton, of Beacon Square, S.W.1., and currently residing at the home of Mr T. Crichton of Roakes Common.

'Correct me if I am wrong,' he began, slightly overdoing the false humility, when his sergeant had noted these particulars, 'but I understand you are the sole individual present without family connections with the deceased lady?'

'With either of the deceased ladies, come to that.'

He jerked his head up, as though suspecting me of levity or worse, and I said:

'There has been a funeral here today, you know.'

'I was aware of the fact, thank you, Mrs Price. We happen to be investigating the death of Mrs Sophie Roche.'

'I only mentioned it,' I said, 'because Miss Stirling's funeral was my reason for being here at all. As you've seen, it was more or less a family occasion and I am not related to them but my husband and I do have rather a special position in the house.'

He heard me out with weary patience while I explained what this was, but he was clearly paying little attention and even signalled to the sergeant not to bother to write any of it down.

'Thank you, Mrs Price. This is all very interesting, but in future I should be grateful if you would confine yourself to answering my questions.'

'I'll do my best.'

'I understand from Mrs Craig that you were with her when she discovered the deceased?'

'Well, not exactly, no.'

'Indeed? Then may I ask why Mrs Craig is under the impression that you were?'

'We'd both been looking around for Sophie, you see, and when I went back into the bedroom where she'd been lying down, Mrs Craig came inside from the balcony and told me about the railing having collapsed and that she was afraid it was Sophie down on the terrace.'

'But you did not ascertain any of this for yourself?'

'No. The important thing was to get to her as fast as possible. She could have been alive, for all we knew.'

'But when you reached her you formed the opinion that she was already dead?'

'I know she was.'

He smiled secretively, as though I had fallen into a trap which had been specially prepared for me.

'And then you went indoors and phoned Dr Macintosh?'

'Yes.'

'You knew that she was dead and yet it did not occur to you to contact the police first?'

'It passed through my mind, but I was in Mrs Craig's house, so naturally I did as she asked.'

'Leaving Mrs Craig alone with the deceased while you were away?'

'Yes.'

'And approximately how long was that?'

'Not more than three minutes. I'd called the number once already today, so I didn't need to look it up.'

'Thank you. And now I want you to think carefully before giving me your answer to this: when you returned, was everything on the terrace exactly as you had left it? And did it remain so until Dr Macintosh arrived, which I take to have been some ten minutes later?'

'Yes to both,' I replied, relieved for some reason which I could not pin down that he had phrased the questions in such a way that I could answer truthfully and yet make no reference to the episode of Margot's hat. 'The only difference was,' I went on, 'that Piers had joined us by the time the doctor arrived. He's Sophie's husband.'

'You're quite certain that was the only difference?'

'Positive.'

I could not swear that he was satisfied, but I knew better than to repeat my denials or throw in any defiant stares and after a short pause he switched to a new tack.

'You knew that she was pregnant?'

'I knew that she claimed to be.'

'Oh? You're implying that it might not have been true? Was she given to prevarication?'

'I wouldn't say that, but she was rather childish and sometimes went to extreme lengths to draw attention to herself.'

'Well, that may be your opinion, Mrs Price, but I can assure you that she was speaking the truth in this instance.

And, in your personal opinion, was there anyone who might have had a grudge against her?'

'Why? Do you mean it wasn't an accident?'

'We have no reason to think otherwise, but we naturally have to rule out the alternatives; and perhaps you would be kind enough to allow me to ask the questions?'

'Yes, of course. The answer to your last one is that practically everyone had a grudge against her occasionally, because she could be such an almighty bore, but I take it that's not quite what you're after?'

'You are correct.'

'Then the answer is no.'

'And you are aware of no suicidal tendencies?'

'Well, there again, I've heard her threatening to kill herself, when things weren't going her way, but I don't think anyone ever took it seriously.'

'I see. Well, thank you for giving me such a full statement. There is one further thing I should like you to do.'

'Oh yes?'

'I want you, if you will, to make a complete timetable of your own and everyone else's movements, so far as you can accurately place them, from the time you arrived here until you and Mrs Craig went out on to the terrace and found Mrs Roche. Would that be feasible?'

'I'll do my best. The trouble is . . .'

'Yes, Mrs Price?'

'I've been here since ten o'clock this morning and surely the relevant time, from your point of view, is after the funeral?'

He gave a slight smirk, as of one who had scored a point. 'Beginning with your arrival at ten o'clock, if you please, Mrs Price.'

'Very well. It may take a little time, but I'll start on it as soon as I get home.'

'Oh, come now! No time like the present, is there? Why not see what you can do while the details are still fresh in your mind? I suggest the morning-room. You'll be nice and quiet in there and I'll see that no one disturbs you. Sergeant, take the lady into the morning-room and then ask Mr Piers Roche if he can spare me a few minutes.'

I left the room with my escort, feeling that, in some unfathomable way, the chief inspector had come out on top after all. Whether his last request was simply a device to keep me under surveillance or whether the entire interview had been leading up to it was something I could not be sure about, but it was plain from his complacent manner that his objective had been achieved.

(iii)

Solitude and fresh surroundings brought a slackening of mood. Sitting at the morning-room desk and staring out on to the terrace, I spent the first ten minutes in a torpor of lassitude. Various isolated images of the day's events bobbed about in my head but the only thing which held my attention for any length of time was the patch of paving, just within my line of vision, where Sophie's crumpled form had lain. Nothing now remained except some smudged chalk marks to show that it had ever been there but I was struck with the picture of that sad, limp figure inside the old fawn dressing-gown, and the fur hat beside it. In a determined effort to dislodge it, I got up and removed myself and my writing materials to an armchair by the fireplace.

With the view from the window now behind me, concentration on the task in hand began to seep through and I unscrewed my fountain pen and put my name and the date at the top of the page. Underneath them, I wrote:

'10 a.m.-10.20 (approx) with Jasper Craig in the morning-room.'

I studied these two breathtaking items for a few moments, then tore up the page and rewrote it, leaving out the approx. It had struck me that since it would apply in some degree to every single entry it would be a waste of man hours to include it, and anyway who was to know or care?

The whole business took more than an hour to complete, partly because I kept remembering incidents out of sequence and had to go back to insert them and partly because I ended by making two neat copies, one for Inspector Mackenzie and the other for Inspector Price, should he condescend to peruse it.

It was while I was copying out the second that I was struck by the revelation which, if not quite on the level of Mr Watt's when he noticed steam issuing from the kettle, certainly gave me a fair to middling jolt. I went mechanically through to the end of the schedule, my mind humming along this new track like an express train, then put the finished work into two separate envelopes, placed these in my bag and sat back to consider the next move. After some deliberation, I decided that it was necessary to begin with a personal inspection of Betsy's room.

There was no one in the hall and the drawing and dining-room doors were both shut. I raced upstairs, silent as a shadow, thinking how simple all this kind of thing was when one struck out with the bold dash, and a moment later gently turned the bedroom door handle and edged my way inside. The slightly depressing pay off was that I could just as well have sailed in banging my tambourine for there were two people in the room already.

One of them was Betsy, who was busying herself with a collection of articles, including a hat-box, which were spread out on the bed. The other, lurking rather obtrusively in the background, was the red-faced young policeman. I also perceived that the verandah door was shut and had a sturdy rope knotted across it.

This called for a somewhat different approach from the one I had mapped out and I said brightly:

'Oh, hallo! I thought you might be here. Can I help?'

'How sweet of you, my lamb!' Betsy said, evincing neither surprise nor mistrust. 'But no, I don't think so. On the whole, we're managing splendidly.'

'Packing up?' I enquired.

'Oh, just a few bits and pieces, you know, which I might need. I'm moving back to the Stables, you see. Well, one could hardly want to remain here and I don't think the chief inspector really wishes me to. So I thought it would be a good plan to get it over and done with, and this nice young man kindly came along to give me a hand.'

'Sure I can't help you with that?' I asked, watching her place about a dozen little round tins in the hat-box, wedging them in with cotton wool and tissue paper.

'You might put your finger on the knot for me. I'm such a mutt at tying up parcels. There now, what have I done with the string? Had it somewhere, I know. Yes, here we are! And could you find some scissors, my love? There should be a pair in the dressing-table drawer.'

'And a good many other things,' I said, opening it, 'Brushes and combs and all sorts. Don't you want to pack them as well?'

'Perhaps not,' she replied vaguely. 'There's no hurry, is there? Some other time will do for them. Now, finger ready? And I'll borrow your pen, if I may, officer dear.'

'It's going by post, is it?' I asked, when this transaction had been effected.

'That's right, my love. They're legally Piers's property now, but naturally he doesn't want to be bothered with that kind of thing at present. So I thought the best way would be to pack them up and send them to his flat. He can go through them when he's ready to. Thank you, constable; it's a lovely pen.'

'A gift from my wife, madam.'

'Oh, are you married? How nice! Well now, Tessa, I do believe there is something you can do for me, after all, if you would. You'll have to leave very soon, I know, so could you send this parcel off for me? The little post office opposite the war memorial stays open till six on Saturdays, and you have to pass it, don't you?'

I didn't as she well knew but, catching her eye, I assented with no hesitation.

'Then there are all these shoes,' she went on with a rush. 'They're so heavy, aren't they? If I were to push them all into one of these plastic bags, would it be any trouble to put them in the car, too, and drop them off at the Stables?'

'No trouble at all.'

'Oh, you are such a dear! Isn't she, constable? And I can manage the rest on my own. Or perhaps Albert will bring them over for me this evening. Let's see, though; you can't carry all this lot down by yourself, can you?'

Having no clue as to what answer was now required of me, I gave none, and she glanced doubtfully at the constable:

'I wonder . . . ?'

'Very sorry, madam,' he mumbled, turning a still more fiery red, 'but I'm afraid I can't help you. Orders are I'm to stay here in this room.'

'Well, of course, and we mustn't think of your disobeying them. I quite understand. Oh, come on, you silly old Betsy, what's the matter with you? I can help you down with the parcels myself. No objection to that, is there?'

'None as I know of, madam.'

'Come along, then. You take that one,' she said, handing me the shoe bag, 'and I'll hump the box.'

I took one of the envelopes from my purse and handed it to the constable, requesting him to pass it on to his chief inspector at the first opportunity.

'All set now,' I said, turning back to Betsy.

'Come on, then. Quick march!'

'I might have guessed he had instructions not to leave me alone in there,' she remarked, as we plodded downstairs. 'Wasn't I a silly old billy not to think of it?'

She sounded genuinely amused and I said: 'Well, perhaps not always quite as silly as you pretend,' and got a sharp look in return.

We placed the two parcels on the passenger seat and, climbing in beside them, I said:

'So they came back?'

'What did, my lamb?'

'The tapes.'

'Oh, the tapes? Now, why should you say that I wonder? What a funny little creature you are sometimes. Drive carefully, won't you, my pet? And try to come over and have lunch with me tomorrow. Robin, too, if he can get away. Goodbye, and thank you again for all your help. The cheese straws were delicious.'

I dumped the shoes inside the Stables front door and then drove round to the war memorial. The post office was still in full swing, as Betsy had predicted, and before putting the parcel on the scales I verified its destination, as to which a certain curiosity had been aroused. It brought a bonus too, for it was addressed to Gerald Pettigrew, Esq., of Barrett and Pettigrew, Essex Street, W.C.2., and it reminded me that I had promised to telephone him for an appointment.

VIII

'DEAR me, yes,' Toby agreed. 'A very terrible affair! Really, one's own troubles quite pale by comparison. I wonder you take it so calmly, but I suppose violent death is a commonplace in your life nowadays?'

'Not at all, and anyway this was an accident.'

'So you keep saying. And a particularly unnecessary one, I should have thought. I mean, what a silly girl to go leaning on a balcony when it was tumbling down! It's not as though she was at all heavy, is it? She must have flung her entire weight on it, wouldn't you say?'

Having after all arrived back at Roakes Common ahead of Robin, I had been obliged to concoct a watered-down version of the day's events for Toby's benefit. To conceal Sophie's death from him was out of the question but I had considered it only prudent at this stage to omit the more sinister aspects, referring to it throughout my account as an accident and cheerfully throwing Dr Macintosh to the lions by hinting that the sedative he had prescribed for her had so dulled her wits that she had lost even the normal reflexes of self-preservation. Unfortunately, owing either to fatigue or lack of rehearsal, I had laid it on too thick and underestimated Toby's fine capacity for separating the wood from the trees.

'Did you ever meet her?' I asked, hoping to steer him into safer byways.

'Once or twice, though we never exchanged many words. Perhaps she didn't know many, if she was as silly as you make out?'

'Well, she wasn't very bright, I agree, but it may not have been her fault this time. I keep telling you she was doped.'

'I know you do, and I must remember to ask darling old Macintosh what he gave her. LSD, by the sound of it. We must put it tactfully though. The medical profession is so apt to be touchy.'

'Have you had occasion to consult him lately?' I asked, grabbing at every straw.

'Oh, he visits me from time to time, you know. I'm rather fascinated by this ulcer of his. Boots have a marvellous new mixture which is supposed to work miracles, and he promised to give it a try. I must get him up here one day and see how it's going. Come to think of it, Tessa, I might kill two birds with one stone, if you don't find the expression too tasteless in the circumstances. That terrible Lulu is always complaining that Harley Street is baffled from end to end by her migraine. I might persuade her to consult him. That should fix her, don't you think?'

'Would she listen to him?' I asked, well pleased by the turn things were taking.

'My darling, she would listen to anything if it was about herself. She is a thoroughly silly woman. Not quite so silly,' he added dreamily, 'as to lean her full weight on a broken balcony, however eager she was to see what was going on below. Tell me, though; how's Piers taking it? Is he out of his mind, poor fellow?'

I gave in. 'Okay, Toby, so he's not exactly prostrated by grief, so far as one can tell, but that doesn't mean he pushed her, does it?'

'I should hope not! Is anyone saying he did?'

'Of course they aren't. It's well known, I admit, that he and Sophie had been on the brink of splitting up dozens of times, but they'd patched things up because of this baby, so why should he want to kill her?'

'Who knows? Perhaps the patching up was more on her side than his. Perhaps he wasn't so eager to be tied down. Anyway, why didn't they get on?'

'I think a lot of it was Margot's fault. She's so damn possessive about those boys. It amazes me that Piers slipped out of her clutches long enough to get married at all. I'm sure Digby will never manage it.'

'Well then, I expect it was Margot who did the pushing. Having failed to break up the marriage by conventional methods, she resorted to desperate ones.'

I shook my head. 'I wouldn't put it past her, but I think you're on the wrong track altogether.'

'You mean, you stick to your story that it was an accident? It doesn't sound as though your surly chief inspector agrees with you.'

'Oh, him! He has about as much chance of getting to the root of it as Mrs Parkes. If he does suspect there's something fishy, you can take it from me that he'll be looking for all the wrong motives.'

'Poor fellow! Why is that?'

'Because it's the wrong victim. If Sophie was killed deliberately it can only be because somebody mistook her for somebody else.'

'Really, Tessa, that sounds even more far fetched than your accident theory. How could they possibly be so unobservant as that? Oh, you mean the dressing-gown? Someone saw a female figure draped in brown camel hair and concluded it was Betsy. Is that it?'

'No,' I said slowly, 'it isn't. At least, you're not doing badly because that was my theory until two minutes ago. I wasn't absolutely thrilled with it because, as you say, someone would have to be pretty daft, or else crazed with the blood lust, to have got near enough to Sophie to give her a shove without realising who she was, but now I see a simpler answer. Oh damn! I do wish Robin would hurry up. It's driving me mad because there's something only he can find out for me and I need it to complete the picture.'

'Well, I expect you're on the right lines,' Toby said kindly. 'After all, you've had so much experience of this sort of thing. If you like, you can tell me about your picture, and I'll say, quite honestly, if I think you're potty.'

'No, I can't do that; not until I'm sure. But it was something you said which gave me this new idea. Just a minute ago, when you were talking about Lulu.'

'Well, that's consoling. It does prove that even the most improbable people can occasionally have their uses.'

'I know, but Robin's the only one who can be truly useful at this stage. Well, never mind, I must just be patient. He's bound to be here soon.'

As I spoke, the telephone rang.

'Bad news?' Toby enquired, when I rejoined him ten minutes later.

'The worst. Robin can't come.'

'How very heartbreaking and annoying for you! Didn't you explain how urgent it was?'

'Yes, but it hardly registered. It's not really his fault, I suppose. His case has tumbled about his ears.'

'Good heavens! That doesn't sound like Robin. I thought he had it all sewn up?'

'They thought so, too. They were absolutely convinced the husband had done it. Now he's gone and handed them a cast-iron, gilt-framed alibi.'

Toby raised his eyebrows. 'How odd to have found it so late in the day!'

'Oh, it was the usual boring thing; the Other Woman, in capital letters. It seems they broke him down on the fact that he did go out again on the night of the murder, but only to visit her, and it was on her account that he'd kept quiet about it. It seems she has a jealous husband and it wasn't until it dawned on them that the alternative was likely to be a life sentence that she consented to tell the police where their suspect had really spent the night.'

'Well, it's nice to know that the age of chivalry is not dead, only buckling a bit at the knees. And don't worry; I am sure it will be the work of a moment for someone as experienced as Robin to rip their story to pieces.'

I shook my head. 'Not a chance, apparently. It's been checked, inside and out, and there isn't a flaw. Also Robin believes the bit about her being scared of her husband. She was practically fainting with terror in case the police should pull him in for questioning, but she still stuck to her guns.'

'How maddening of her! Well, as I see it, you have but two courses open to you.'

'Name but one.'

'In the first place you could hop over to Dedley and crack the case yourself, thereby releasing Robin for more important duties.'

'You kill me, Toby.'

'In the second, you could stop on here for a few days, while he battles it out on his own, and sort things out at this end. I am quite willing to play my small part by telling you all the silly things I can think of about Lulu.'

'I doubt if it would help. I'm really stuck now, and I must say it's a bit galling to think of a murderer stalking around the Rectory and getting away with it every single time.'

'You told Robin about Sophie?'

'Yes, but I don't know that he took it in. He's so cross with himself for galloping along this false trail and hitting nothing but a blank wall at the end of it. It's hardly surprising that one female more or less falling off a balcony doesn't count with him at the moment. His only reaction was that two deaths at the Rectory in five days was beginning to look a bit unhealthy and that I should keep as far away from it as possible. That's a big help, considering I'm expected there for lunch tomorrow.'

'But you agreed to cancel that, no doubt.'

'I temporised, if that's the word. I said I'd more or less promised Betsy and I couldn't very well let her down.'

'No, I doubt if temporised is quite the word for that.'

'Well, it was in a way because I added something else.'

'Oh yes?'

'I said it would be quite safe to go because you'd agreed to come with me.'

'Oh, thanks awfully, Tessa.'

'It's all right, you'll be in no danger. I'll tell you something which I could have told Robin, if he'd been in a mood to listen. Nothing is going to happen while Margot and the others are back in London.'

'You're confident of that?'

'Completely.'

'Very well,' Toby replied. 'In that case, I will give your proposal due consideration.

IX

(i)

OPTIMISM rose again with the sun and, lying in bed on Sunday morning, I formulated and discarded about fifteen different schemes for tying up the loose end in my theory about Sophie's death. By the time Mrs Parkes entered with the coffee and newspapers I had hit on a plan which despite some hit and miss elements seemed to offer a fair chance of success.

'Another gorgeous day?' I suggested, surveying the patch of forget-me-not blue framed in my window.

'Good old storm coming up, by the feel of it,' she replied, unloading her precious cargo on to my bed.

Mrs Parkes could truthfully be described as an optimist by nature, for she was fond of small disasters and tireless in predicting them.

'Mr Crichton's not feeling too good,' she went on. 'Doesn't know if he'll be able to get up today.'

'What's the matter with him?' I enquired, ripping through the pages to Hobson and Co.

'Couldn't say. He's a nasty colour, though. Think you ought to call the doctor?'

'Not just yet. We'll give him an hour or two and he may improve.'

'Hope for the best, I suppose. Wouldn't be much of a holiday for you, if he was taken really bad.'

'You're so right,' I told her, 'but I don't think it will come to that. I believe I know just the cure for him.'

I had to wait until I was up and dressed before putting my plans into action because Toby's phobia about the telephone decreed that the one and only instrument be situated in the most inconvenient place he could dream up, which was the darkest corner of the hall. Nevertheless by ten o'clock I had dialled the Storhampton Police Station and asked to speak to Chief Inspector Mackenzie. I was informed that he was not available and invited to state my business.

'It is in connection with the death yesterday of Mrs Sophie Roche,' I replied, slipping into the jargon. 'I have certain information to put before the chief inspector, if he could spare me a few minutes.'

Various underlings then attempted to trap me into parting with the information but I wasn't having any and they grudgingly consented to convey my message and ring me back.

In anticipation of this, I had armed myself with copious reading matter, so as to remain within inches of the telephone during the interval, but there was only a ten-minute lull before it burst into life again. The chief inspector would see me in his office at eleven-thirty.

I gathered that he was breaking into a family Sunday morning specially to accommodate me and there was a hint in the air that my information had better be good. I therefore spent a few more minutes putting the finishing touches to the story I proposed to tell him.

'You're supposed to be a nasty colour,' I said, 'but you look much the same as usual to me.'

'Appearances are deceptive then, because I am far from well. I'm afraid it would be madness to think of going out. I hope you're not too disappointed?'

'But, Toby, you surely don't expect me to go on my own, after what Robin said? It was practically a sacred pledge.'

'I had hoped you might abandon the outing. In fact, I don't quite see how I can manage here without you. Mrs Parkes won't stay a minute after twelve on Sunday, you know. There are no exceptions to that rule. I could be dying, for all the difference it would make.'

Pretending to be temporarily baffled by the problem, I said thoughtfully:

'No, you obviously shouldn't be left on your own. Looking closely, I see that your colour is a little bit nasty, but on the other hand, how can I let poor Betsy down? Look, as it's an emergency, couldn't you overcome your prejudice against Lulu just for an hour or two? I'm sure she'd be only too willing to drop everything and dash over to sit with you. I'll just run down to the telephone and put it to her. Shan't be long.'

His colour really did take on a nasty tinge at this point, and his words were not very pleasant either; but I had him in a stranglehold and he knew it. In a very short time he had begun to feel slightly better.

'Don't rush it,' I advised him. 'I'll go ahead and explain that you'll be along later. About twelve-thirty or so, right?'

'If you insist.'

'Good. We meet again at Philippi.'

(ii)

I took a roundabout route to the police station, which was in the market square, on the principle of easing out every stone, the better to turn it over quickly should the need arise, and a series of detours were involved in establishing the whereabouts of No. 2, Mayfield Drive.

It proved to be one of a collection of detached bungalows which had been run up in the past four or five years, and it had a cheerful, well-groomed look about it, as befitted its owner's profession.

As it was in a cul-de-sac, I had to back and turn in rather a confined space to get out again. I was releasing the handbrake for about the fifth time when I saw a woman emerge from one of the neighbouring bungalows. She was a nondescript, middle-aged type of person, and yet something about her so arrested my attention that I clean forgot what I was doing and the car rolled backwards again and struck the pavement. This led to a prolonged and disagreeable altercation with another woman, who had had the mischance to be exercising her dog on the pavement behind me, and it was a near miracle that they had not both been crushed to death between the fence and my back bumper. By the time the recriminations and apologies had been repeated several times and we had parted on relatively civil terms, the first woman had naturally passed out of sight. Since I had already discovered that Mayfield Drive was but one tentacle of a positive octopus of walks and crescents and squares, there was nothing to be gained by going after her. Moreover, I was now in danger of being late for my appointment with Inspector Mackenzie.

*

As it happened, I arrived on the dot, but despite this he received me churlishly, only half rising from his chair as I went in and glancing sideways at his watch even before I had sat down. He then brought out a pipe and after a lengthy filling and lighting operation asked me if I had any objection.

'None whatever,' I answered untruthfully. 'And I hope you won't think I'm wasting your time. Did you get the schedule I wrote out for you, by the way?'

'Yes, Mrs Price. My men are quite efficient, you may be surprised to hear. Thank you for doing it so promptly though. Perhaps a bit too prompt, was it? You've had second thoughts and there's something you wish to add, is that it?'

'No, not exactly.'

He sucked his pipe for a bit and then said:

'Let's try and sort this out, shall we, Mrs Price? You are saying that you are satisfied that the document you handed to my constable was correct in every detail?'

'As near as I could make it.'

'Then may I ask why you have requested this inter-view?'

'It was to tell you of something which had no place in that schedule, and so it was only afterwards that I saw that it might have some significance.'

'Oh yes?' he said, suppressing a yawn.

'It was something I noticed on the day before the . . . accident.'

'At the Rectory?'

'Yes.'

'So you were also there on the previous day, were you? How did that come about?'

'I called in on Mrs Craig on my way down from London and spent about an hour with her.'

'And what took place during that time? Let's see, Friday it would have been. Miss Stirling having died the previous Wednesday, I understand?'

'Yes, but nothing actually took place. It was just a small thing I noticed, without attaching any importance to it at the time, but which might be relevant, in view of what happened yesterday. At one point, when Mrs Craig was talking to her sister on the telephone, I went out on to the morning-room terrace. I happened to look up at the balcony of Mrs Craig's bedroom, which is directly above, as you know.'

A fraction more alertness had crept into the Chief Inspector's manner and there was a new attentiveness in his eyes, telling me that I had struck the right note, so I continued without a break: 'You remember that old vine?'

He nodded.

'It covers part of the wall outside the morning-room and it has also grown sideways along the balcony. I noticed that one of the main stems on that section had broken off and was hanging loose. You couldn't have seen it as I did, because after Sophie's accident more chunks had naturally got broken as well.'

'That's quite interesting, Mrs Price, but is it really all you've come to tell me?'

'Can't you see what it means?'

'I can think of a variety of explanations. Perhaps you would tell me which one you had in mind?'

'Surely, that if someone had been fooling about with the balcony rails, that broken stem practically proves it was done before the day of the funeral, maybe even three or four days before. The break didn't look particularly new.'

The pipe had gone out, but he did not relight it. He placed it on his blotter and then, putting his elbows on the desk, locked his fingers together and looked at me in what I feel sure can best be described as a quizzical manner.

'Well now, Mrs Price, I've no doubt you're quite sincere in your belief that you've unearthed some valuable information, but there's just one thing that puzzles me. What leads you to think there is any suggestion of someone having tampered with the balcony rails?'

'Because you as good as told me so,' I replied.

'Oh, come now, I can't allow you to get away with that.'

'Not in so many words, but while I was making your time and motion study it dawned on me that its only conceivable purpose would be to show who had the best opportunity to spend an unobserved quarter of an hour on the balcony, either before Sophie went up there to rest, or while she was asleep.'

'Go on,' he said. 'This is entertaining, if not instructive.'

'It was also a fairly safe bet that you had privately asked each of us to draw up a similar sort of timetable, so that by co-relating and comparing them you might narrow it down even further, and maybe sift out the truth from the lies.'

'What a mind the woman has! It's not such a bad idea, at that. Pity I didn't think of it myself.'

'Well, not really, Inspector, because if you had thought of it it wouldn't have done you any good, would it?'

'Would it not?'

'No, because I've just pointed out that any monkeying about on the balcony was almost certainly done at least twenty-four hours before the funeral and conceivably even before Miss Stirling died.'

He picked up the pipe again, but only to beat out a gentle tattoo on the desk.

'Well, I'm grateful to you for coming along to tell me all about it, Mrs Price. It may not be quite so world shaking as you appear to believe, but it's always nice when members of the public volunteer to co-operate, and I hope you'll let me know if you get any more bright ideas.'

It was a grudging acknowledgment, to put it mildly, but there was enough substance in it to indicate that my hunch was probably right, and as I was leaving the room he wrapped it up for me.

'Oh, by the way,' he said, with a studied casualness which any first-year drama student could have knocked spots off, 'there is to be an inquest on Tuesday. I don't expect you'll be called. After all, your evidence could only be a corroboration of Mrs Craig's, couldn't it? All the same, I'd like you to be present, if you don't mind; just in case.'

X

(i)

HOPES of my blackmail being a hundred per cent successful were severely dashed when I parked the car in the Rectory drive and looked in vain for a venerable green Mercedes.

'Toby hasn't turned up?' I asked Betsy. I had met her coming from the kitchen garden with a trugful of lettuces and we were walking up to the Stables together.

'No, but he's on his way. He telephoned to say he'd be a little late. I'm glad really, because I've got something rather horrid to tell you. Oh, don't look frightened, my pet. I shouldn't have said that, because it's nothing like the really horrid things that have been happening. Just a little disturbing and unpleasant.'

'And, by a strange coincidence, I have something to tell you. Who's going to begin?'

We had arrived at the long, single-storey brick-and-flint building which now formed the elegant Craig residence and Jasper came out of it, heavily slung about with cameras and tripods. He gave me a smart tap on the behind, tweaked Betsy's hair and strode off towards the river, looking highly delighted with himself.

'Dear old Jas,' Betsy said, gazing fondly after him. 'He does so revel in this weather.'

'Name one who doesn't.'

'I mean for his work, my dearie. Just look at that sky! Perfect shooting weather. He hates to lose a minute of it and this is the first real opportunity he's had to get out there since the day Mamma died.'

'He's surely not planning to set up anything before lunch?'

'Gracious, no. Once he makes a start, he'll be gone for hours. No, he's just loading up the punt with all his gear, so as to be off the minute lunch is over. Let's sit out of doors, shall we? It's so heavenly.'

The stable yard had been turned into a garden, with lawns and rose beds. There was an old clock tower at one end of this quadrangle and a fig tree in the opposite corner. Altogether an ideal place in which to while away half an hour on Sunday morning and I assented gladly.

'That's right, my pet, and we'll have a nice, cold glass of wine. You'd like that, wouldn't you? Could you bring a few chairs out for me? I did ask Jasper to, but, poor love, he can't think of anything except work in weather like this.'

'Who's going to begin?' I asked again, reaching up and nipping off a fat green fig which I had a whim to sample with the champagne.

'Perhaps you'd better, my duck. You always manage to say your piece so concisely. My stories are rather apt to get out of hand, as you may have noticed.'

'I can certainly be concise with this one. In a word, I saw Albert's wife this morning.'

Perhaps I had overdone it, for she did not seem to be exactly bowled over.

'Did you, my pet? Where was that?'

'In Storhampton. She was coming out of one of those new little houses behind the hospital.'

'Well, fancy that? Did you speak to her?'

'Didn't get a chance. What do you make of it, though? I thought she was supposed to be in Devonshire?'

'Oh well, I expect she's come up for the day to see a friend or something.'

'Oh, come off it, Betsy. People don't go to all the trouble of eloping with tobacconists and then return a few days later just to see a friend.'

'Well, I don't know, I really don't. Everything seems to have become so strange and horrid all of a sudden. It's a pity you didn't speak to her, because then you could have asked her yourself, and I'm sure you'd have found she had a perfectly good reason for being here. But we'd better not mention it to Albert. It might upset him.'

'How is Albert today?'

'A little better, I think. At any rate he's offered to see to the lunch for me. That's a blessing, isn't it? My cooking's not up to much, as you know, and I felt rather nervous when you told me you were bringing dear old Toby.'

The subject of Albert's wife having been thrust aside as one of life's annoying little mysteries, I recalled that Betsy had something rather more momentous to relate in exchange and I asked her to begin at once. Immediately she looked troubled again and the poor, long suffering handkerchief came in for a stint of pulling and twisting.

'Yes, you're quite right, my lamb, I've been putting it off. We've been having such a nice chat and it seemed a shame to spoil things, but I've got to tell you. It's about your ring, you see.'

'What ring?'

'The one Mamma left you in her will. I was so pleased about that, you know. She really thought a lot of you, and she believed you had great talent, too. The fact that she wanted you to have her very special ring proves it. That's what makes this so particularly disagreeable.'

'Makes what? I'm not with you, Betsy.'

'No, I always begin at the wrong end, but it's like this: since Mamma wished you to have it, I thought it would be a nice idea to get it out of the safe and give it to you today. Oh, I realise, even I realise, that there are all sorts of tiresome rules about probate and so on but I thought Gerald could probably square that for us. Or, if the worst came to the worst, you could lend it back to me when they came down to do the valuations. The point was, it seemed ridiculous to leave it lying in the safe when it might be working for you and bringing you all sorts of valuable offers. Don't you agree?'

'Yes,' I admitted, much impressed by her practical view of the situation.

'So, first thing this morning I went over to the house and unlocked the safe. You remember that little wall safe at the back of the linen cupboard?'

'I do indeed. I always thought it was rather a clever place to put it.'

'Well, I suppose so, although it was a nuisance having to pull all the bath towels on to the floor every time Mamma wanted something taken out or put back which, as you know happened rather frequently; and then the insurance people made us have that extra lock on the door which was another bother. However, to come to the point, when I opened it up this morning, I am dreadfully sorry to tell you that the ring wasn't there.'

She evidently expected this news to send me into screaming hysterics and I do confess to a rather lowering sense of disappointment, but of the two of us she was far more distraught and to console her I said:

'Oh, don't worry about it, Betsy. I'm sure there's some very ordinary explanation, like Maud sent it to the bank or something.'

She shook her head. 'No, my lamb, that's right out of the question. She would never have been parted from that one. In fact she almost always wore it, right up to the time when her poor fingers got so thin; and even then she liked me to fetch it for her sometimes so that she could hold it and look at it. Besides, I haven't told you about the other things.'

'Oh Lord! You mean there are other things missing as well?'

She frowned. 'I couldn't be positive about that. It did seem to me that there was rather less in the safe than there should have been, but it's true that Mamma kept all her most valuable stuff at the bank, so I could be mistaken. No, what I'm chiefly worried about is some of the things that are there. I'm terribly afraid they're copies.'

'Oh gosh, Betsy!'

'Yes, I know. What first put me on to it was that, when I couldn't find your ring, I began checking through the rest and I discovered there was something wrong with one of the bracelets. Or rather, there was nothing wrong with it which was the whole trouble.'

'Sorry, but I've lost you again, Betsy.'

'It's my fault because I explain things so badly, but it was simply that there used to be a stone missing from one of her bracelets. Quite a tiny one, you'd hardly have noticed it, but, it fidgeted her dreadfully and she was always on at me to get it repaired.'

'Only you never did?'

'I meant to. It was wrong of me, but there were so many more vital things to worry about just then and I kept putting it off. But, you see, my darling, when I took it out this morning the stone was back in place; and I'm pretty sure it's a fake and that all the others are too. Of course, I'm no expert so I could be wrong, but then how could the stone have got back all by itself?'

'Have you told Jasper?'

'Good gracious, no, my pet. Whatever made you think I would? Jasper despises everything of that kind and he knows even less about jewellery than I do. No, I shall just have to wait until I go to London tomorrow. I've got to see Gerald and I must somehow find time to go along to Mamma's own jeweller afterwards.'

'What about Albert?'

'What about him?' she asked sharply.

'I just wondered whether, knowing how you're apt to put things off, Maudie might have asked him to get the bracelet repaired for her?'

'Oh no, dearie, that's most unlikely. If she'd asked him to do a thing like that, he would have consulted me first; I'm certain of that. And I'm definitely not going to mention it to him, if that's what's in your mind. He might imagine I was hinting all sorts of things. Now, what's become of darling old Toby, I wonder? He should be here by now, surely? Oh Lor! You don't suppose he's waiting for us over at the house? We'd better go and look. Just as well, really, because we're having lunch over there. It makes things easier for Albert, our kitchen being so teeny. Oh dear, and I promised to take him the lettuces, didn't I? Come on, Betsy, old girl, wake up!'

'Have the others gone back to London?' I asked, as we bustled through the stable yard towards the house.

'Yes, all except Dickie. He's gone to stay with friends somewhere near Newbury. They came over and fetched him. Rather grand people, by the look of them. Piers and Digby were both going to spend the night at Lowndes Square. They wanted me to go with them. Margot was quite annoyed when I refused, and Piers was most insistent about it too. When I wouldn't go he was all for staying on here, so that I shouldn't be alone. Very sweet of him, but of course I said no. Sometimes they quite seem to forget that I've got a husband to look after,' she added a trifle wistfully.

'But I suppose they'll all be back on Tuesday for the inquest?'

'Oh yes. At least, I'm not sure about poor old Dickie, but Margot and the boys are coming tomorrow night. I can't tell you, my love, how glad I shall be when the nasty old inquest is over and we can begin to get back to normal.'

As it happened, normality was about the last thing I anticipated as being in store for her, but she was looking harassed and unhappy again and I had no wish to add to her troubles. Nor, for the time being, did I make any further reference to the bracelet. It had not escaped me that the mention of Jasper in that connection had left her totally unruffled and slightly amused; whereas as soon as I had introduced Albert's name she had shot off at half a dozen tangents and done everything possible to divert me to other topics.

(ii)

During lunch, which was served to us by a sombre, though now sure-footed Albert, Jasper invited Toby to accompany him about half a mile upstream, where he had constructed a hide from which to photograph the flight of the wobbling wagtail, or some such creature, over the ancient walls of a ruined abbey which was prominently featured in his current film.

It was hardly the kind of afternoon's spree to appeal to Toby, even in the most favourable circumstances, and he looked rather nonplussed, signalling an S.O.S. in my direction and saying:

'I don't know whether I will or not. I shall think it over.'

'Don't strain yourself,' Jasper said. 'It's nothing to me.'

'The thing is,' Toby explained, 'I wasn't feeling very well this morning. It might be wiser to stay away from the water for the time being.'

'I wasn't suggesting that we should punt across the Atlantic, my dear.'

'I should go,' I said, nodding at him in a marked and vigorous fashion. 'The fresh air will do you good and you're not likely to be seasick on a day like this.'

'Yes, do, my honey-bun, it will do you all the good in the world to be out of doors and you'll be so fascinated to see Jasper at work. Personally, I could never have the patience for it and he always says I ruin everything by talking at the wrong moment; but you're so nice and taciturn, Toby dear.'

'Very well,' he agreed, going down before this barrage. 'But I shall fetch my hat from the car. I have to be careful about sunstroke.'

'I will come with you,' I said. 'I think I left some sunglasses in your glove compartment.'

'What's the matter with the pair you were wearing before lunch?' Jasper asked.

'Nothing, but I've dropped them somewhere,' I replied, dropping them under the table.

'You can come with us, if you like,' he informed me. 'So long as there's no prattling.'

'That's awfully kind of you, Jasper, but I'd better not. Betsy tells me you're away for hours when you get out there and I promised Robin to be home by four. He means to try and get over to Roakes for an hour or two.'

'Now what have you got me into?' Toby asked morosely, as we stood together by the Mercedes. 'I am not cut out for dangerous living and, quite apart from that, you know very well that Nature bores me almost as much as Art.'

'No, it doesn't. At least, you love being on the river and if you can get Jasper into a man to man mood you might pick up something valuable.'

'Except that if one of the men happens to have poisoned his wife's milk and pushed somebody else over a balcony, the other man might find himself on a sticky wicket.'

'Well, if he should shove you overboard you'll just have to swim to the bank, but I don't believe there's the slightest risk of it. The fact that he invited me to go as well practically proves that he has no dishonourable intentions. Furthermore, I take the view that we are all perfectly safe from this murderer, whoever he may be, so long as none of the rest of the family is around.'

'So you've said before.'

'And shall go on saying. But, meanwhile, if Jasper does get at all chatty, you might pump him as to whether he knew in advance about the terms of Maud's will; and, if so, whether he mentioned it to anyone else.'

'I promise nothing,' he replied grimly. 'The whole enterprise fills me with deepest gloom.'

'Never mind,' I told him. 'You must just keep reminding yourself that even the most boring old ruin is probably preferable to Lulu.'

For once, Betsy did not try to detain me, seeming quite anxious in fact to speed me on my way, although she did ask me to be a lambkin and come back on Tuesday to accompany her to the inquest. I said nothing of the instructions I had already received on this matter, but suggested that we might also drive to London together the following morning.

'What about Albert's wife?' I asked, just before we parted.

'Well, I don't really see there's anything we can do, my pet, even if you did see her. She has a perfect right to come and go as she chooses, and I daresay you were mistaken, you know.'

'Yes, but I was thinking of your mother's jewellery. After all, she's supposed to have pinched a mink coat. Perhaps she raided the safe, while she was at it.'

Betsy coughed and looked down at her shoe, which was tracing patterns in the gravel. 'The fact is, Tessa, I've been thinking about that and I believe we may all have got it wrong. I shouldn't be at all surprised if Mamma had said she could have the coat. She was rather given to impulses of that kind, you know; and then sometimes she regretted them, which made things a bit awkward for everyone. Well, let's say she told Albert's wife she was going to make a codicil to her will, leaving her the mink, but she forgot to mention it to anyone else and died before she could do anything about it. So, of course, Albert's wife would have known that she had no legal claim and perhaps she was afraid none of us would believe that Mamma had promised it to her, so she told her tobacconist friend about it and he put it into her head that she should take it and they'd do a bolt together.'

'Why would he do that?'

'Oh, I don't know, Tessa, but it was insured for four or five thousand and perhaps he was rather greedy. He looks it, you know. Quite a shifty sort of person, and he may have thought he could persuade her to sell the coat and get enough money to set up in business somewhere else. I daresay she would do that sooner than lose it altogether. Don't you think that's a much more likely explanation than her eloping for love? He's really such an unattractive little man, you know; not nearly so nice-looking as Albert.'

I could have named several wild improbabilities in this story, not least that the proceeds from a fur coat of dubious origins, however heavily insured, would hardly set up much of a business, in Devonshire or anywhere else; but it would have taken a very mean spirit to puncture one of Betsy's cosy little fantasies, and I did not argue. With renewed promises to telephone in the morning and arrange about our trip to London, I turned the car round and drove back to Roakes.

XI

(i)

IT IS weird how the most flaming lie can sometimes turn into stark truth. When I arrived at Toby's house I found Robin already there, tapping his feet and vindicating my every word. It was as well that I had prevailed upon Toby to accompany me to the Rectory and I virtuously explained that I had left as soon as the river party set forth.

His mood had turned rosy again for they had found a new lead in the Dedley case, which looked promising. However, as it led them straight to a newly-opened hairdressing shop in the High Street, where the murdered woman had been employed, nothing constructive could be done until Monday morning and he was taking the rest of the day off.

He declined to tell me more than this for which I was thankful, being anxious not to lose my grasp on the various threads which formed the pattern of events at the Rectory, and it was gratifying to find that he was now just a little more inclined to pay serious attention to them.

I began with a resume of my interview with Chief Inspector Mackenzie and at the end of it he said:

'So you assume from his reaction to your story about the vine that they are treating it as murder?'

'That was my impression; although if it was, it must have been designed for someone else. It was sheer fluke that Sophie was on the scene at all.'

'Was it? I can think of several ways she might have been lured there. However, I presume you think the trap was actually laid for Betsy; and all that remains now, I suppose, is for me to get round Mackenzie to confirm that the post really had been sawn through?'

'That was what I wanted from you yesterday but I've progressed since then. Betsy was vehement about the balcony having been in a rocky state all along, but I had my doubts. For one thing, she didn't mention it until about ten minutes after we'd discovered the accident, and as she's for ever rambling on about every trivial thing that comes into her head, I find it highly peculiar that she should have kept a little matter like this to herself. Even if that surly old chief inspector had told me that I was on the wrong track, I shouldn't have been entirely convinced, but in fact he did nothing of the kind. He never actually denied that the balcony had deliberately been made unsafe.'

Robin said thoughtfully: 'So what it comes to is that there have been two separate attempts on Betsy's life, neither of which succeeded. First of all the wrong person drinks the poisoned milk and then the wrong person falls off the balcony. We've got a singularly inefficient murderer on our hands, haven't we?'

'Not necessarily. It's the hazard that comes from operating by remote control. Fate steps in, as you might say.'

'Very well; leaving aside the method, which seems to have been extremely slapdash, what about motive? Who chiefly stood to gain by Betsy's death?'

'Well, that's the crux, isn't it? There's Jasper, of course. He's obviously bored and irritated half to death by her sometimes, but they've been married for over twenty years and they probably suit each other pretty well. The truth is, he's on a good wicket with Betsy. She gives into him all along the line, worships the ground he treads on and never utters a word of criticism. I don't know whether she minds secretly about his rudeness and his infidelities and so on, but outwardly she positively encourages him to go his own sweet way. All in all, he'd be much worse off without her.'

'Except financially, of course. She's now a very rich woman.'

'Oh, I know, but whatever money she owns would be his for the asking. And if it was the loot he was after, Betsy dying before her mother would have done him no good at all. I don't know how much she was worth in her own right, but I bet it wasn't a quarter of what she's inherited now.'

'Whereas, if Betsy had pre-deceased Maud, which seems to have been the plan, Margot would have had most to gain, with Piers and Digby coming in next and Dickie and Sophie about halfway down the batting order. Though personally I'd be rather inclined to discount those two entirely. I can't really see old Dickie going in for anything so ill bred as murder, and although Sophie wasn't too bright, she would hardly have been idiotic enough to lean on a balcony which she had personally rendered unsafe.'

'No, but she might have been witness to something connected with the poisoned milk, which made her a danger to the murderer. Even if he didn't originally set up the balcony trap for her, he might have snatched the opportunity of using it, when by an unforeseen chance she was alone in Betsy's bedroom.'

'Enticed her on to the balcony and then persuaded her to lean over? It would have presented quite a problem.'

'Not an insoluble one though, Robin. He could have made any old excuse to get her out there, then manoeuvred her into the right spot, applied the quick shove and over she'd have gone. She was pretty frail and feeble at the best of times.'

'It would be quite a help to know which, if any of them, knew in advance about the terms of the will. So far as one could tell, they were all completely flabbergasted but one shouldn't count too heavily on appearances with that bunch.'

'I know,' I agreed sadly. 'I've got Toby working on that very point, but I doubt if he'll come up with anything. The trouble is, I have a feeling that what evidence there was has now been destroyed.'

'Evidence?'

'On the recording tapes. Betsy must have known or guessed that one of them was red hot, because she locked them away in her wardrobe. But somebody forced it open and presumably removed at least one of them. She's posted the rest to Gerald Pettigrew now, but that's a case of shutting the stable door if ever I heard one.'

'I don't see the purpose of removing the tape, though. I suppose you're implying that it contained a record of the interview Maud had with Pettigrew when they discussed the terms of the will he'd brought down for her to sign?'

'Right. Betsy told me her mother was crazy about that machine. It was one of the few toys that she didn't grow bored with. Don't you think she'd be liable, in her rather fuddled state, to leave it running whether she was speaking into it or not? If somebody had played it back afterwards, he would have known all about Betsy inheriting. Dr Macintosh had warned them that Maud might pop off at any moment, so there was no time to work on her to revoke the will. The best hope lay in bumping off the chief beneficiary.'

'Nevertheless, it was still unnecessary to steal the recording. It might have told the murderer what he needed to know, but it wouldn't have given his identity away to anyone else.'

'Unless his voice was on the tape as well. How about that, Robin? Supposing he had gone into Maudie's room when Gerald left, having overheard part of their conversation, and spoken to her. At this point he has no idea that the machine is switched on but later he realises that it was and that it would be a dead give-away to anyone who played it back.'

'Well, that puts Jasper on the spot again. Wasn't it established that the rest of them didn't arrive until after Gerald had gone back to London, and that Betsy was out at a meeting during his visit?'

'Yes, but it doesn't have to be true. Digby was supposed to have been at some folk music festival, but that must be about the hardest alibi of all to crack. And one of the others could have left the race-meeting for a while, pretending afterwards to have been in one of the other enclosures. It's not more than half an hour's drive from Newbury. Betsy was safely off the premises and if Jasper is speaking the truth he was out on the river all day. So no one need have known if one of the others had turned tip, perhaps for some quite innocent purpose, although afterwards he'd have had the best of reasons for keeping quiet about it.'

'Albert might know.'

'Yes, he might, but I have to tread warily there. I have a feeling that Albert is involved in something shady, and Betsy, for some reason best known to herself, is shielding him.'

I repeated the story of Maud's jewellery and Robin said:

'I suppose Albert knew about the safe in the linen cupboard?'

'We all did, including Albert's wife. We were always being chivvied off there to fetch her this and that. It was only designed as a precaution against burglars from outside. Anyone inside the house could have helped himself whenever he chose.'

'And you think that's what this pair have been doing?'

'It's more logical than the story of her taking off with the tobacconist, don't you think? That strikes me as distinctly far-fetched, specially as I now have grounds for believing that she's not in Devonshire at all. Also it would account for Albert going to pieces like he has. What he's suffering from, in my opinion, is not grief but fright.'

'Because he thinks the game may be up?'

'Specially now that he's inherited this whacking great legacy. Even assuming that he had disposed of the jewellery and stashed the money away in Belgium, it wouldn't be worth a quarter of that tax free two thousand a year. I don't suppose that in fact Maud would have prosecuted, but if she'd found out that Albert was fleecing her, she'd have had Gerald down there in a specially chartered helicopter, wheel chair and all, to cut him out of her will.'

'And the most likely way of Maud finding out was through Betsy?'

'So Albert might have reasoned, and furthermore he had the best opportunity of all for dosing the milk. Anyone could have done that, actually, because it was always left standing in the pantry from dinner-time onwards; but all the same, filling it was his job and he was jolly quick off the mark in washing it out before anyone had time to examine the contents. He also had the best opportunity for sawing through the balcony posts.'

'And you're still convinced that both attempts were directed at Betsy?'

'Well, isn't it obvious, Robin?'

'Not entirely. I can see someone might have wished it to appear like that, and I can also see how that same person wouldn't have genuinely wanted either attempt to succeed, which in a sense they didn't, even though two people have died.'

'What are you driving at?'

'Well, take the episode of the milk, for a start. I'll accept that it would have contained something dangerous enough to kill Maud, but it wouldn't have taken much to do that, in the state she was in. Also she doubtless took it in combination with other drugs, which could have made it that much more lethal. But would it really have worked on a strong woman like Betsy? Isn't it more likely that someone was out to create the impression that an attempt had been made on Betsy's life, but in fact took good care to ensure that the dose was only strong enough to make her slightly ill?'

'There's no telling what effect it would have had if she'd drunk the lot. She claims that she wouldn't have noticed anything wrong with the taste because of that malty stuff she always mixed into it; so presumably it could have been a fatal dose, even to someone in normal health. But are you really hinting what I think you are, Robin? If so . . .'

The protest which had sprung to my lips had to spring backwards again because there was an interruption. Robin had made a warning gesture towards the door, to indicate that Toby had returned, and unfortunately he was not alone.

(ii)

It was true that her hair was snowy white and another distinctive feature was her voice, which trilled up and down the scale with no particular application to what she was saying, sometimes fluting out into a little-girl treble, at others descending to a throaty saloon-bar gurgle. Although plump and fortyish, she had a flirtatious manner and baby blue eyes which she used in rather an arch way and I could see why Toby lived in terror of her.

'Oh, he's a terrible old grump, that cousin of yours,' she announced, patting the sofa as an invitation to seat myself beside her. 'The trouble I have with him, you'd never believe! Now, this is specially between you and I, Tessa. I may call you Tessa, mayn't I?'

'Oh, please!'

'That's right, dear. I knew from what Toby told me about you that we'd get along like a house on fire. I've got a sixth sense where other folk are concerned, and you may not believe this, but I really enjoy a little feminine natter sometimes. Now, boys! No need to listen in to what we're saying. This is a private matter between Tessa and I. Well now, dear, how about you and me entering into a little pact?'

I guessed what was coming and said rather priggishly:

'I should warn you that I have no influence whatever over Toby and I don't know anyone who has.'

She sighed. 'You don't have to tell me, dear. Obstinate isn't the word. But it's so bad for him to be shut up inside himself, isn't it? Personally, I get so much happiness through helping others and familiarising myself with all their little problems. Don't you find that?'

'Yes,' I admitted. 'As a matter of fact, I do.'

'There you are! I could tell we were birds of a feather. What I want you to do is to persuade that wicked cousin of yours that I'm not a designing female on the lookout for a husband. I'm quite contented with my lot, as it happens. I've been lucky enough to know great love and happiness and I have my precious memories. But that's no reason why we shouldn't be good pals and neighbours, is it? We pass this way but once is my motto, so why not try to spread a little joy as you go?'

Somewhat flummoxed by this Fairy Truegold speech, I was searching for an adequate reply, when Lulu leaned away from me and raised her voice to include Toby and Robin, who were muttering together by the window.

'I've been explaining to your little cousin here that I'm not the scheming harpy you take me for, Toby.'

'Oh, good!' he said politely.

'And she's on my side, I can tell you that. I'm sure you are too, Mr Price. With all your experience of the wickedness of this world, wouldn't you say that to cut yourself off from your fellow-men is the worst crime of all?'

'No,' he replied, looking perplexed. 'I can't say I would.'

One way and another, it was beginning to look like the most public private pact I had ever been invited to take part in, but as Robin and Toby had instantly resumed their conversation. Lulu was thrown back on a little more of her chosen feminine company.

'So you're an actress? Do tell me about yourself. It must be such a wonderful life. I expect you'll laugh, but I've always had a special affinity with stage folk. I don't know why it is, but we always seem to hit it off. I daresay you've heard of Maud Stirling, the famous singer, who died just the other day?'

'Yes, indeed.'

'One of my closest friends. She spent quite a lot of time down here, you know; at Storhampton.'

'Yes, I know.'

'Never shall I forget going there one morning, when she'd opened the grounds to the public. It was such a scream because one fool of a woman who'd paid to come in mistook her for the help or something and, would you believe it, asked her where the loo was? Old Maud didn't turn a hair. She was a marvellous mimic, you know, as well as being such a great operatic person, and she went straight into the most killing imitation of a cockney char and told the woman which way to go. I'll never forget how we laughed about it afterwards.'

On balance, I rated this anecdote ninety per cent apocryphal, so mumbled some stray remarks about Maud being an old family friend and, catching on, Lulu said thoughtfully:

'Of course, she was before my time. I never heard her in the flesh, so to speak; only on records, although it's wonderful what they can do with those nowadays. It was her daughter who was my real friend.'

'Margot?'

'Is that her real name? We always call her Betsy.'

'Oh, her! She's a dear, isn't she?'

'You can say that again! And a lovely sly sense of humour. I'm always telling her she ought to have been on the stage, but she says she'd be hopeless because she wouldn't be able to remember a single line.'

This sounded authentic enough and I said: 'Have you known her long?'

'Oh, ages and ages, dear. When my hubby was alive, we lived at Storhampton, you know. Quite a big old place, up by the golf club, but I've always had a hankering for the real countryside. And one or two jolly, friendly neighbours are as good as a dozen, any day,' she added a trifle wistfully.

'But you're still able to keep up with the old Storhampton lot?'

'Now and again. I'm turning into a real country bumpkin these days, but I still do my Family Planning work. They're such a good crowd. That's how I first met Betsy Craig.'

'Oh yes, she's very keen on all that.'

'Me too. Wouldn't give it up for anything. Second Tuesday of the month, come hell or high water. Some of those poor women who come to us, you wouldn't believe the things they say! It's wicked to laugh, I know, but I've got a very keen sense of humour and I never can resist seeing the funny side. But I mustn't talk about myself. When are you coming over to see all the little improvements I've made at White Gables? Not that it wasn't a lovely, old world place, mind you, but it did require a lot doing to it, and I've had an aviary built on the patio. I'd love you to see it. How about tomorrow lunch-time?'

'It's very kind of you, but I have to go to London tomorrow.'

'Oh, what a shame! Something to do with your acting?'

'No, mainly to get my hair washed.'

'Oh, but there's no call to go all the way to London for that, dear. We've got the most marvellous new man just opened in Dedley. I always go there now and there's no one more particular than me about hygiene and that. You really should give them a try.'

Nothing will ever alter my conviction that Robin possesses an extra pair of ears tucked away inside his skull and he certainly had them switched on then. Moving away from Toby in a rather trance-like fashion, he picked up Lulu's glass and, having refilled it, sat down in an armchair at right-angles to her, turning on the rueful smile.

'Tessa always would have it that Dedley was pure desert for things like hairdressers, but I often suspected that she was simply making excuses to go to London and spend a lot of money. I must say,' he went on shamelessly, 'you do give the lie to her story.'

Lulu bridled delightedly and would doubtless have tapped him with her fan, had she been holding one.

'Now, now; naughty, naughty! You won't catch me letting down my own sex. We poor women must stick together. I was just the same once upon a time, always popping up to London to the hairdresser. But I'm a changed person now. José's got this really smart place in the High Street, and of course he's straight from Mayfair, which makes all the difference. I don't mind admitting that I wouldn't go anywhere else now.'

Apparently there were a good many other facts on the subject which she didn't mind admitting and she went rattling on for a good ten minutes about wonderful old José, with only the minimum of prodding from Robin. Evidently, it did not cross her mind that there was anything bizarre in his passionate interest in feminine coiffure, but Toby was more sceptical.

'I quite see what he is up to, Tessa,' he said, manoeuvring me to a distant part of the room, 'but I cannot imagine what he expects to get out of it.'

'Oh, just filling in some background, you know. It has been known to produce something constructive.'

'He must be raving if he's hoping for anything constructive from Lulu. She's oblivious to everything that doesn't directly concern herself.'

'And there, Toby, I fancy you under-rate her. From my brief acquaintance with Lulu I can tell you that she is positively brimming over with useful tips.'

XII

MRS Parkes was granted her thunderstorm in the end, though she may not have been pleased by its timing, for it started clattering around our ears in the small hours of Monday morning.

I was awakened by distant thunder growing closer with every burst and, when that had died petulantly away, the rain, which had been shivering in the wings, swept forward with a soughing sigh and pounded down on the baked earth.

The temperature had dropped so dramatically that I had to get out of bed to shut the window and retrieve my eiderdown from the wardrobe, where it had been stacked away during the heatwave. This woke me up conclusively, but I did not despair, for I possess numerous remedies for insomnia and on this occasion there was just the right kind of mechanical, memory-testing task all ready and waiting. This consisted of taking myself back, step by step, through the schedule I had made for Chief Inspector Mackenzie and its purpose was the one which I had boldly attributed to him. However, I trust he found it more rewarding in this respect than I did, for I went out like a light somewhere around ten-thirty a.m. on Saturday, with Piers coming into the kitchen to make his light-hearted report on Sophie's threatened miscarriage.

The garden next morning was a desolate sight, with branches and windfalls tossed around on the grass and every bed strewn with mushy rose petals. I visualised Mr Parkes being in a sorry humour, for, like so many people whose activities are governed by the weather, he is constantly outraged by any misbehaviour in this department. Nevertheless, I plucked up courage to relay through Mrs Parkes the request that he should put up the hood of my car.

'Yes, that's the trouble with these contraptions,' she remarked. 'Up and down, up and down, all through the summer. I shouldn't want the bother of it.'

'I quite agree with you,' I said. 'It's the bother of it which I find detestable too. Let's hope Mr Parkes doesn't see it in the same light.'

Having put this matter in train, I next tried to telephone Betsy, to find out what time she would be ready to leave. I rang the Stables first and got through to Jasper, another of those outdoor workers who had failed to cultivate a philosophical attitude to the climate. His reaction to the storm was quite simply that he had been singled out by the heavens for an act of personal spite, although there was an underlying hint that I was not entirely blameless in the matter either.

'Do you realise,' he demanded furiously, 'that I only needed two more days for my last shots? Five hundred feet in the can and I'd have been home and dry.'

'Very trying for you,' I agreed, 'but it was ever thus, was it not? I know when we do exteriors on location we count ourselves lucky to get four hours sunshine in a fortnight.'

'I daresay you do,' he snarled. 'And with your commercial budgets I can see that you could laugh it off. It's slightly different for me.'

I was tempted to remind him that it was not so very different, now that he had Betsy's quarter of a million to play with, but at the same time I wasn't looking for insults so I said:

'What about all the editing and printing? Why not get on with that instead?'

'Mainly because you're holding me up with your idiotic chatter. What do you want, anyway?'

'To speak to Betsy, if she's there.'

'No, she's not. At least, she was until a minute ago, dithering about and getting in my way, but she seems to have gone now. Probably over at the house.'

'All right, I'll try that. And, if she's not there, I expect Albert will know where I can find her.'

'No, Albert won't, because he's here, washing up the breakfast things. Which reminds me; Betsy said something at breakfast about spending the day in London. That's probably where she's gone.'

'I don't think she'd have done that without letting me know, Jasper. We were supposed to be driving up together.'

'I don't know anything about that, but I confess I wasn't really listening.'

'Well, if you see her, will you ask her to call me back? It's important.'

'Not to me,' he replied. 'But I'll tell her if I remember.' I dialled the Rectory number, but no one answered. Half an hour later there was still no word from Betsy and no reply when I tried the number again. I was driven to the conclusion that she had forgotten all about our engagement and gone to London by train.

I did not enjoy my solitary journey, for the rain cascaded down in buckets the whole way and the other drivers were as moody and irritable as I was, feelings which they expressed by overtaking me at ninety miles an hour and throwing up bathfuls of greasy water on to my windscreen. Long before I reached the tail of the traffic crawling over the Chiswick flyover I was bitterly lamenting having tied myself down to a twelve o'clock hair appointment but it was too late for regrets of that sort and in fact decisions involving deep rooted strategy now had to be faced.

I had intended to go directly to Beacon Square, park the car there and inject myself back into the mainstream with a few telephone calls before setting out by taxi for the next leg but, between them, the weather and Betsy's absent-mindedness had set me so far behind that, to add to all the other woes, I was now committed to a long, losing battle with the traffic wardens.

However, there is nothing to compare with the scented, womb-like shelter of a really expensive hairdressers to create the illusion of well-being and an hour or so in the company of Mr Jackie, senior partner of Jacques et Gils, always restored the drooping spirits.

Unlike Mr Gils, who is an authentic Parisian and rather intimidating, perpetually staring with smouldering, coal black eyes at his own reflection above the client's head, Mr Jackie is a gregarious and sentimental Englishman, with a passion for mild indiscretions, particularly those appertaining to his more celebrated clients. He received me rapturously, being agog for news about the Stirling funeral and where the money had been left.

Maud had been an old and much-prized customer and even Betsy went to him three or four times a year, but Margot was unpopular in the shop, on account of her stinginess. She was always trying to trade on her mother's standing to get cut rates for herself and had even been known to wash her hair at Lowndes Square, wrap it in a scarf and march into the shop, demanding to have it set. Jackie was not at all put out to learn that she had virtually been cut off with a portrait.

Sophie, on the other hand, had patronised a rival establishment, so his curiosity about her death was minimal and I was able to bundle this incident safely into the background.

'What a terrible shock, though!' he said, reverting to Maud. 'That golden voice stilled for ever, as you might say. Poor old darling, dropping off like that, without any warning. Frankly, Miss Crichton, I expected her to outlive us all, truly I did. Such sparkle! I was down there only the previous week, you know.'

'She was okay then, was she?'

'Bright as a button. We had a lovely chat.'

'Well, she was pretty rocky some of the time, by all accounts.'

'Oh, I know, but I always thought that spirit of hers would carry her through for a good many years to come. That's what I find so sad, if you see what I mean? Her dropping off the hook like that when she was still enjoying life and planning for the future. We were making a new creation for her, you know. That's what I went down about. She wanted a fitting before we did the final trim on it. That shows you, doesn't it? She was a regular tartar for having things perfect, you couldn't help admiring it. Luckily, she'd kept a few wisps of her own in front, so we were able to get the hair-line looking natural. Some people might call it silly vanity to worry about such things at her age, but I'm all for it. I think it shows the right attitude to go on caring how you look right up to the end, don't you?'

'Certainly I do, and I must say you did a beautiful job for her. I never knew.'

'Not a soul did, apart from Mrs Craig, of course. But that's what we call professionalism, isn't it? Mind you, I'd never have breathed a word, even to you, while she was alive. She'd have had me boiled in oil, most likely; but it can't harm her now, poor old duck. The wig's finished now and it's a real beauty. I'll show you, if you're interested. Not that it'll ever be worn, and so bang goes a hundred and fifty quid down the drain. Still, I'm not moaning about that, truly, Miss Crichton. It's losing poor lovely Miss Stirling that upsets me.'

'But, Jackie, you don't have to lose financially as well.'

'No? Well, I can't see Mrs Roche coughing up, can you? Anyway, I wouldn't want her to find out what the money was for, and I know she wouldn't rest until she'd got it out of me. And I wouldn't sell it to anyone else, if they went down on their bended knees. You'll think I'm touched, I daresay, but to me that wig was just as much a part of Miss Stirling as if it had grown on her naturally.'

'But since Mrs Craig was in the secret, why not speak to her?'

'Oh, I wouldn't want to worry her, would I, with all she's going through. I know so well what it's like, from when I lost my own mother. No, I shall just have to keep it as a memento of happy days gone by,' he said, brushing away a tear. 'There we are then, that's you done! I'll just get Shirley to slip the net on, if you don't mind.'

He was clearly too moved to make it a suitable time to pursue the matter, but while I was under the dryer it occurred to me that I had something more practical than sympathy to offer, for Gerald Pettigrew's address and telephone number were written down in my diary. I fished it out of my bag, copied the details on to a blank page and wrote underneath: 'Miss Stirling's solicitor and executor, who will settle all accounts in strictest confidence.'

My plan was to hand this to Jackie before I left, so that he might profit by it when emotions had cooled, but meanwhile the first idea had given birth to a second, and as soon as Shirley released me from the dryer I asked her to bring me a telephone.

The switchboard operator told me that Mr Gerald was engaged with a client and put me through to his secretary. I explained that I had been requested to fix an appointment and after a bit of swishing back and forth through the engagement diary she marked me down for eleven a.m. on the following Friday. Pretending it was an afterthought, I then asked if the client with Mr Gerald was by any chance Mrs Craig, and she said no, it wasn't.

'Strange!' I mused. 'I was certain she was due to see him about now. We were to meet for lunch afterwards. I hope I haven't made some ghastly mistake.'

There was a brief pause, while the mind on the other end of the line made itself up, and then the voice said:

'As a matter of fact, Mrs Craig did have an appointment this morning, but she hasn't turned up. We tried to contact her in the country, but there was no reply, so perhaps she's on her way. Should I give her any message if she does arrive?'

'It doesn't matter,' I said. 'I may call again later, to see if you have any news.'

I gave the torn-out page to Jackie, who remarked that he hated to be mercenary, but supposed one had to live. The mood had changed during the interval and he was once more the full, dedicated artiste of the haute coiffure, endlessly twitching and tweaking at my hair, as though putting the finishing touches to a wedding cake, until I could have snatched the brush from his hand and flung it across the room.

'Going somewhere nice for lunch?' he enquired, evidently sensing my impatience but misinterpreting it.

'No,' I said. 'As a matter of fact, I'm going straight back to the country. Something tells me there isn't a minute to lose.'

XIII

BY ONE of life's hideous ironies, it was Albert who found her. On him of all people, whom she had striven so hard to shelter and protect, she had perpetrated the worst outrage of all. Almost the cruellest part of it, as he tried to explain to me in an English which had suddenly fallen apart, was his impotence to cover her indignity from the prying eyes of strangers, for he knew that he must not disturb the naked body which lay stretched out in the bath, nor even put a hand in the water which covered it; and that everything, including the red-hot bars of the electric wall fire, had to be left exactly as it was for the police.

The story which led up to his dreadful discovery eventually emerged as follows:

Having finished washing up the breakfast dishes at the Stables, he had been obliged to remain there for a further fifteen or twenty minutes because Jasper had needed help in moving some tins of exposed film which he intended to spend the morning developing, and in blacking out the bathroom to make a temporary laboratory. It was therefore half past nine or thereabouts before he returned to the Rectory. On his way upstairs he had passed by Betsy's room and through the open door had seen her London clothes laid out on the bed. The door of her bathroom was shut and he could hear the water running. He had continued upstairs to his own flat on the top floor, presumably to do a little quiet brooding, for it was nearly ten-thirty before it occurred to him that he had heard no sounds from below and, stranger still, that Betsy had not called out to say goodbye to him and let him know what time she would be home.

So downstairs again he went and found the bedroom door open, just as before, and her clothes still lying on the bed. There was no sound of running water from the bathroom, signifying, although he did not know this until later, that the taps were already submerged; and there was no response when he tapped on the door. He tried the handle, but found it locked.

At this point a slight panic must have set in for, instead of going to fetch Jasper, he had gone out to the garage to find the tall ladder, meaning to try and climb in through the bathroom window. However, for some inexplicable reason the ladder was not in its usual place and still more valuable time had been wasted in a fruitless search for it. He estimated that it was around eleven o'clock when it finally occurred to him to enlist Jasper's help, and by that time the stable door was open and the horse had trotted off to the pub. Albert had then returned to the Rectory, stopping off at the woodshed to collect an axe and, although almost fainting with terror, had managed to hack his way in through the bathroom door.

The remaining details were filled in some hours later, after the police had completed their gruesome business. Albert, by then, had been treated for shock and despatched to his own quarters. Meanwhile Jasper, having walked in during the middle of the third act, had at first refused to believe what had happened and then collapsed on the staircase in a storm of sobs, literally wailing like a child for its lost mother.

Even before I turned into the drive I knew that I was too late and that the terrible forebodings which had sent me hurtling out of London had all been justified. There were two police cars parked outside in the lane and two more inside the gate. Dr Macintosh was standing beside his own car, talking to one of the officers as I drove in. I was trembling so violently that it was an effort to move, but when I finally staggered out of the car he walked over, grabbed my arm and led me at a brisk pace to the morning-room. There, in brief and factual terms, he told me that Betsy was presumed to have died between nine and ten o'clock, although it was difficult to establish this with complete accuracy because the intense heat from the electric fire had kept up the temperature of the water, interfering with the normal onset of rigor mortis. He also told me that the actual cause of death was drowning, but the water and taps had been heavily charged with electricity and there could be little doubt that in getting into the bath she had received a severe enough shock to render her unconscious.

When I asked him how such a thing could have happened he tried to explain to me about short circuits being conducted by water when the wiring was faulty, as had been found to be the case with the two bathroom plugs, one connecting the fire and the other the towel rail, both of which had been switched on.

'Which means that someone messed them up deliberately?'

He shrugged. 'That's for the police to find out, if they can. It could have been accidental. Amateurs can be mighty careless about electrical equipment. Still, it's odd that they should both have been wired up wrongly.'

'And it could have been done days ago, without causing harm to anyone, so long as the hot weather lasted?'

'Suppose so, but that's not our worry, is it? Take things one step at a time, that's my principle. They're bad enough without our trying to delve into all the sinister implications, even if they have to be faced in the end. Margot's on her way down, incidentally.'

It was a curious incidental, in view of the reflections which had prompted it, but I let it pass and he told me that the police had arranged for one of their men in Knightsbridge to go round to Lowndes Square and break the news and that Piers had telephoned half an hour later to say that they were leaving London immediately in his car. Dr Macintosh then told me that he had personally been in touch with Gerald Pettigrew and, judging by the poor chap's reactions, he considered himself to have had a sight more unpleasant task than the Knightsbridge policeman.

'Is Gerald coming down too?' I asked.

'Not immediately. I'm to ring him this evening to let him know what . . . um . . . the arrangements are. He's sending one of his junior partners to Sophie's inquest tomorrow.'

When his ghastly tale was done, he stood for a while with his back to me, jingling some coins in his pocket and staring out on to the terrace, and I guessed he was rehearsing his speech about there being nothing I could do by hanging around and should now pack it in, go home and try to stay out of mischief. It would not have been the first time he had delivered it, but on this occasion he turned back to me with a worried look on his face, and said:

'Look here, Tessa, you appear to be taking this very calmly. It's unlike you and I hope it's not deceptive. Quite right to keep a grip on yourself up to a point, but if you feel like breaking down, go ahead and don't mind me. I'd rather that than have another case of shock and hysteria on my hands.'

'No,' I said slowly. 'Somehow, for once in my life, I don't feel like crying. Perhaps that'll come later, because I was devoted to Betsy, as you know, and she was very, very kind to me. Tears would be a relief, in a way, but they won't come. What I feel now is more like a mixture of rage and hatred.'

'Now, now!' he said warningly.

'Oh, don't worry. I'm perfectly calm, I promise you. It's a cold rage and I mean to keep it that way. I'd give anything I possess to have the foul beast who did this put behind bars, and I'm not going to let emotions get in my way.'

'That's all very fine talk, Tessa, and if it helps you to let off steam, so much the better. But take a tip from me and don't go around breathing fire and vengeance and trying to get after the murderer yourself. Leave all that side of things to the police.'

I felt too sunk in despair, just then, to argue with him, so nodded and, after giving me another steady look, he went on:

'On the other hand, if your nerves are in as good shape as you say, and you want to make yourself useful, there's one quite practical job you could do right away.'

'That's good. What is it?'

'Nothing heroic, I'm afraid. Just stick around here till Margot arrives. It shouldn't be more than another half hour, but I don't awfully care for the state Albert's in. Jasper too, come to that, although he's probably numbing his sorrow with a bottle of whisky by now. Albert's different. I couldn't get him to take a sedative and I wouldn't put it past him to do something foolish.'

'I'll be glad to stay, for as long as you want me to, but I hope you're not hinting that I'm to restrain him forcibly from committing suicide?'

'No, I'm not, otherwise I wouldn't leave you alone here. He's suffering from shock, that's all. It'll wear off, but what he needs now is to get some of it out of his system. If you go up and chat with him, it'll probably do the trick. I'd stay myself, but there's not much I can do.

Physically, there's nothing wrong, and I've got patients waiting for me at this minute who are in a much worse pickle than he is.'

'All right, I'll do my best. What about Jasper, though? Are you prescribing any therapy for him?'

'No, I should leave that job for Margot. Jasper's not the kind to bottle things up. Quite the contrary, as you might say, ha, ha!' he added, smiling sourly at his own joke.

Thus it was that I heard the full account from Albert and, by no means for the first time, I had to applaud Dr Macintosh's diagnosis. The simple truth was that Albert had spent twenty years in a matriarchy and communication with women came naturally to him. To be deprived of their society, their sympathy, advice, exhortations and demands was an alien condition and only increased his obsessive remorse about Betsy's death and his own failure to prevent it.

Not that it was all plain sailing to begin with, for I found him slumped in an armchair in his sitting-room, with a black crochet shawl round his shoulders, and he looked cold, as well as frightened and unhappy. Guessing that his dreadful experience had created a mental block where electrical appliances were concerned, I casually switched on the radiator, and when, rather to my own surprise and relief, I did not instantly drop dead, he began to respond to my overtures and was soon launched on a tide of incoherence, in which he repeated himself, told me things in the wrong order and occasionally lapsed into French. It was only when I had the notion to make him some coffee that the real breakthrough was achieved and he got firmly into his stride.

I was aware that the accepted remedy in this kind of emergency was strong, milky tea, with lashings of sugar, but I guessed that this did not apply in Belgium, and compromised by adding the sugar and a dollop of milk. It was while I was fetching the milk from the refrigerator that I was struck by a teasing memory and at the very end of our interview I asked him another question which, so far as I knew, had no direct connection with Betsy's death. I was a shade apprehensive about the effect it might have on him, but we had become such buddies by this time that it was worth the risk.

'Tell me, Albert,' I said, stirring my own coffee, which was black and unsweetened. 'Do you remember the day of the funeral, when you came into the kitchen carrying the bunch of flowers which you'd intended to put on Miss Stirling's grave?'

He nodded but shifted his eyes away and I sensed a return of the former tensions.

'You put them in the refrigerator, didn't you?'

'Yes. What has this to do . . . ?'

'And that was because, after you came in, you saw me watching you from the pantry?'

'No, I saw nothing,' he said sullenly. 'I put the flowers in the refrigerator so they would stay fresh. You remember I told you this.'

'I know you did, but I've got what they call a photographic memory and there was something about the way you were carrying them. It's fixed in my mind and it's been puzzling me. You may think this is none of my business, but what else were you carrying, Albert, which was covered by the flowers and which also went into the refrigerator?'

The expression on his face when I put this question startled me so badly that my hand shook and some coffee spilt on to my dress. I stood up and began scrubbing at it with a tissue, not looking at him.

'There is a cloth in the kitchen,' he said dully, 'I will fetch it for you.'

'No, don't bother. It will wash out and I've got to go now, anyway.'

Ignoring this, he got up and went into the kitchen. I followed a few minutes later and found him standing perfectly still and staring down at the table.

'There was nothing,' he said, without looking up. 'Only some flowers. You imagined the rest.'

'Okay,' I said. 'I only came to tell you I'm going now. Mrs Roche will be here very soon, so you won't be alone. But listen, Albert, if you do know anything, or possess anything which might count as evidence, there's no obligation to tell me about it, but I do beg you not to keep it from the police.'

He did look up then, staring blankly back at me, as though not understanding a word, but the baffled innocence act did not convince me in the least. I had seen his face when I first broached the subject and I could not get away fast enough.

XIV

'SO THE burning question is,' Toby announced, 'who gets all that lovely money now?'

'Is that really the burning question? I can think of several other fairly hot ones.'

'Well, I've always understood that financial gain is the most popular incentive in affairs of this kind. I imagine Robin will bear me out?'

'Not always, but quite frequently it is,' Robin admitted.

'And there is certainly quite a whack to be lost or gained here.'

'That's the whole trouble,' I said.

'I think what Tessa is trying to say is that the issue is not sufficiently clear-cut for us to ascribe that particular motive to any one person for all three murders.'

'Thank you, Robin, it is exactly what I was trying to say; and that's not all. Apart from not knowing the murderer or the motive, we don't even know for certain who the intended victim was. There have been three altogether, but which one was he really after?'

'Three deaths, but not necessarily three murders,' Toby objected. 'You could postulate one natural death, one murder and one accident, or any other permutation you care to name.'

'I don't care to name a single one. It makes our task far too complicated, and my kite flying with Chief Inspector Mackenzie demonstrated without any question that the balcony had been deliberately fixed. So there's one murder for you, even if it wasn't meant for Sophie. Also, from what Dr Macintosh said about those electric plugs, one can't possibly write that off as an accident either. And there is a curious feature about that episode which I should like to draw your attention to. It, too, could have been aimed at Sophie. There's no saying whether the bathroom had been fixed by the time she used it, or how likely she would have been to plunge into the bath in the middle of the afternoon, but all the same it's a coincidence one shouldn't ignore.'

Robin said: 'To go back to Toby's argument, though, you still haven't demonstrated conclusively that there were three murders, and I don't see how you ever could. Not even an exhumation would prove it in Maud's case because a dose which might have been lethal to her wouldn't necessarily have killed a healthy woman like Betsy. The results might tell us that we were dealing with a rather inefficient murderer, but there would be no proof either way.'

'Then I'll manage without that kind of proof. I've suspected from the very beginning that there was something fishy about Maud's death, and everyone I've spoke to since has expressed surprise that she died when she did. I'm certain that Betsy was uneasy about it too, however much she may have pretended otherwise. Jasper was slightly taken aback too, by the sound of it, although he might have reasons for denying that now.'

'Come to think of it, I suppose if you wanted to kill someone a good way of covering your tracks might be to start by removing two other people for whose death you had no motive at all,' Toby suggested. 'But it does seem rather callous.'

'Perhaps a process of elimination might clear some of the ground? To begin at the beginning, so unlike my dear wife, the first attempt could only have been directed at Maud or Betsy. Are we unanimous about that?'

'No,' I replied, 'we're not. The only circumstance in which it could have been intended for Maud was if Betsy was the murderer, which you were hinting at yesterday, in your oblique way. I couldn't disprove it then, but Betsy's death rules it right out.'

'Very well. So it means that unless Toby's theory is true and that two unnecessary murders were committed in order to mask one necessary one, Betsy was the intended victim all along?'

'Which is exactly what I have always believed, so it's comforting to know that intuition and logic can sometimes march hand in hand.'

Toby said: 'And all that remains for us is to decide who had the strongest motive for disposing of Betsy. Since the general view seems to have been that she was an angel straight from heaven, it shouldn't be too hard to find the exception; excluding myself, I need hardly add.'

'Did you really dislike her as much as you always pretended?'

'Well, no, perhaps not quite as much as that, but she was a little too goody-goody to be true. One felt that in its way it was just as much of an act as Margot's ridiculous pretensions to noble birth. They both overdid it. However, I know you don't agree with me, and really it's beside the point. Even if your view of her was the exceptional one, people don't get themselves murdered simply for being poseurs, so we'll need to find a stronger motive than that.'

Robin said: 'Such as Toby's burning question: who has the most to gain financially?'

'Yes, and in my view, that's where we're really up against it,' I told them, 'because the greed motive wouldn't apply to the same person throughout the series, even supposing the murders were planned in the order they occurred in, which hasn't yet been established.'

'It's a bit of a tease,' Robin admitted, 'because, if Betsy had died before her mother, Margot, Piers and Digby would probably have come off best. Whereas, the way things have turned out, Jasper becomes the principal beneficiary, assuming that Betsy has left everything to him. Once Maud was dead, the best hope for Margot and the boys was to keep Betsy alive, at least until she'd been prevailed upon to make some provision for them, which she undoubtedly would have done.'

'Now that you mention it, I believe Piers and Margot made some effort to get her to go up to London with them after Sophie's death, Piers especially. But she refused point blank and I suppose he could hardly drag her away by force. Also he might have thought that the risk wasn't all that acute. She'd already moved back to the Stables and it was only on account of the storm that Jasper was working indoors and using their bathroom. And if it hadn't been for the storm, you know, which no one except Mrs Parkes was expecting, Betsy wouldn't have needed to switch the heating on. There'd have been plenty of opportunity for rewiring the plugs to make them safe again when they all came down for Sophie's inquest. What's happened about that, by the way? Will they postpone it now?'

'No, they're going ahead,' Robin said. 'But it will be adjourned to allow the police to continue their investigations, as the saying goes.'

'I'm glad to hear it,' I told him. 'It will give me time to continue with a few investigations of my own.'

'I don't awfully like the sound of that. What had you in mind?'

'Well, there's Albert, for a start. I'm not sure what he's up to, but obviously he's dead scared about something, and I would never be surprised if his wife were involved as well. I think I'll pay a call tomorrow. I'm sure people who live in these new little housing estates take a keen interest in their neighbours' comings and goings, wouldn't you agree?'

'Yes, I would,' he replied. 'And nor do I overlook the possibility of Albert taking a fairly keen interest in your comings and goings. If he happens to be a triple murderer, I daresay he wouldn't jib at one more. Personally I consider you'd do far better to come over to Dedley and spend a nice, uneventful day with me. With any luck, I'll have cleared up most of my business by lunch time.'

'I can't do that, Robin. I've been commanded by the chief inspector to attend the inquest. Even though it will be just a formality, I imagine that still holds, specially as they now won't have Betsy's evidence. In any case, I don't honestly believe that Albert is capable of murder. He hasn't the nerve, for one thing. That imperturbable act was a very thin façade, you were right there. He's more like a jellyfish than a Jeeves these days.'

'Guilty conscience, perhaps?'

'Could be. I feel he knows something which he dare not pass on to the police, for fear of it's all coming out that he's been up to something shady. I have an idea there's someone who might be able to throw a little more light on it, but I promise I won't set foot in the Rectory, or the Stables either.'

This undertaking partially reassured him and it happened to be a promise which I fully intended to keep. In one or two trivial respects, however, I may as well confess to a slight equivocation. If, as seemed likely, Albert's was the hand behind the faked jewellery and if, as I also supposed from her vehement denials, Betsy had known this, then who had a stronger motive for wishing to dispose of her? The fact that she would have covered up for him for ever, rather than risk 'unpleasantness', counted not at all in his favour, for he was obviously a person of mean intelligence and fright had made him stupider still. Furthermore there was one feature which put Albert in a class by himself. If my understanding was correct, he alone possessed a motive which was in no way modified by the order of events. Whether Maud was alive or dead, and whether Betsy inherited a fortune or a pittance, made no difference at all. She was and would have remained a constant threat to him until the day of her death.

XV

'HALLO! I've seen you before, methinks,' she said brightly, and her words fell on my ears like the sound of a waterfall in the desert. Familiar now with the route, it had taken barely fifteen minutes to drive there from the Town Hall, even including a brief stop at a chemist's shop; not nearly long enough to concoct a plausible reason for the stiffness in my left wrist, which was now wrapped in a crêpe bandage.

During the short time at my disposal I had churned over various opening remarks, only to fall back at last on the decision to leave it to the inspiration of the moment. It was a rather feeble conclusion, for I had a feeling that the success of my interview would depend largely on the opening stages, and her greeting had got me over the first and most formidable hurdle.

'It's quite likely,' I replied. 'I've been around these parts for some time. We used to live in the gardener's cottage at the Rectory.'

'Did you now? Before my time that must have been. Ron and I have only been here the one year. No, it was last week I saw you; in Dedley of all places. Now what was it called? *Safari*? Some name like that?'

'*Sirocco*?' I suggested. 'Was that the one?'

'You're right, you know. *Sirocco* it was. On at the Regal. We often go there Monday nights. It's the one evening when Ron's mother can baby-sit. Well, fancy meeting you in the flesh! And you lived at the Rectory? That's how you came to know Miss Stirling, then? Dreadfully sad her dying, wasn't it? I felt really cut up. She was such an old dear, always ready for a laugh; you'd never think she was so famous.'

Things were improving by the minute and Mrs Chalmers had only to continue in this strain for a little longer and there was a fair prospect of my finding what I sought without even the bother of removing the bandages. Hopes soared higher still when she said:

'Look at me, though, keeping you standing out here gossiping! Come along into the lounge. Would you care for a coffee? It wouldn't take a moment.'

'Lovely!' I said effusively. 'If you're sure it's no bother?' She was a moon-faced, wide-hipped woman of around thirty-five, with springy, dark hair, lively intelligent eyes, and an air of relentless cheerfulness which overflowed into the little room she led me into. It was slightly over-powering, as a matter of fact, because the bright chintzes on the chairs were flowery and old-fashioned, whereas the curtains derived from a later era and were printed all over with watering cans and vegetable marrows. The gardening motif also extended to the rest of the room which was crowded with potted plants in lattice design plastic containers.

However, it had been over-optimistic to expect that we should get through the session without some reference to my injured wrist, and when she returned with the coffee she cordially invited me to describe my symptoms. I had to confess, as she pressed and pummelled, that the pain was not excruciating, and she gave it as her professional opinion that I was suffering from a slight sprain, adding merrily that it was as well that it was my left wrist, as otherwise people might get some funny ideas. She also advised me to leave the bandage off since it had most likely served its purpose, with which I entirely agreed.

'The fact is,' she told me, 'I don't take on private patients, as a rule. I get as much work as I can cope with at the hospital. Miss Stirling was a special case, but now that she's passed on I've got these free periods and when you told me on the phone that you were a friend of hers, I thought: "Right-ho, that's Fate, then," but now that I've seen it, Mrs Price, I don't think there's much I can do for that wrist of yours. It wouldn't be fair to pretend otherwise. It'll clear up in no time, you mark my words, and massage isn't going to help one little bit. Not that I'm not flattered that you thought of consulting me, because I am, and I don't know what Ron's going to say.'

'Did you visit Miss Stirling every day?' I asked, accepting another cup of coffee.

'Except for weekends. I used to look forward to it. To be honest with you, there wasn't a great deal I could do for her either, but it cheered her up, and then again she'd been used to massage all her life. Didn't feel right without it, she used to say, poor old soul.'

'So you must have been with her only a few hours before she died?'

'Yes, and it's funny about that. I remember saying to Ron that she seemed so cheery that day. I just couldn't believe my ears when I heard on the eight o'clock radio that she'd gone. Less than a week ago! Doesn't seem possible somehow.'

'Still, I suppose elderly people often cave in very suddenly?'

'Gracious, yes. You don't have to tell me that; and she was up and down like mercury. And then that other poor creature falling out of the window, only a few days afterwards! Her niece, would it be?'

'Grand-daughter-in-law.'

'That's right. A real chapter of accidents, you might say.'

I gathered from these reflections that neither the eight o'clock radio nor the Storhampton grapevine had so far reported the third death at the Rectory, so did not refer to it either, but said:

'I've just come from the inquest.'

'Have you, really? What happened?'

'Nothing much. A police officer gave his report and then there was the medical evidence, which was purely technical and over my head. After that, the coroner adjourned for a week, to give the police time to find out how it happened.'

'Poor chaps, I wouldn't want their job. Poor girl, too! You knew her, I expect?'

'Not very well. It was really Miss Stirling and Mrs Craig who were my friends.'

'Funny that, when you think of the different age groups. Still, Miss Stirling was one of the lucky ones who stayed young in heart, as I often used to tell her. She loved to be surrounded by young people too, and that's a sure sign. None of that carping and complaining you get from some of our senior citizens. In fact in my view she rather spoilt that grandson of hers. What was his name?'

'Piers? Digby?'

'Piers, that's the one. Always put me in mind of Southend. We didn't see so much of the other one but this Piers was often there, specially the last few weeks. He was very fond of his grannie, by all accounts, and so handsome, isn't he? You couldn't find it in your heart to say no to him.'

'Was he there the last time you went?'

'Might have been, I don't recall. But her solicitor was, I do remember that. Poor chap!'

'Oh, of course, you witnessed the will, didn't you?'

'Little knowing, as you might say. And then they got Maureen in for the other signature. Can't you fancy another biscuit?'

'I'd love to, if you're sure . . . ? They're so good.'

'Go on, help yourself. You look as though you could afford to put on a bit of weight. Still, I suppose you have to be very strict with yourself in your line of work.'

'Maureen was the day nurse, was she?' I asked, cramming down yet another biscuit.

'No, that was the other one, I forget her name. Miss Stirling just used to call her Nursie and so did Mrs Craig. Quite a middle-aged sort of person, she was, and inclined to be bossy, if you know what I mean, when there were too many visitors. No, Maureen was the night nurse.'

'But she was on duty on Wednesday, the day Miss Stirling died?'

'No, she wasn't. Can't have been, because the other one was there too, but Maureen was always hanging around in her off-duty hours. These young things don't need much sleep, I suppose, and from what I know of Miss Stirling she wouldn't have been the kind to keep her dancing attendance all night. The fact is, she made rather a pet of Maureen. I expect it was because that Piers got on so well with her; always giggling together over that tape recorder thing. I didn't care greatly for her, personally. She was pretty enough, I grant you, but an eye to the main chance if ever I saw one. Sometimes I thought Mrs Craig should've put her foot down; and as for her training and knowledge, well, I wouldn't give you tuppence.'

'How did you get on with Albert?'

'The manservant? He was polite enough, but I didn't have much to do with him. Bit snoopy, I'd say, but then some of these foreigners are. His wife was quite a pleasant sort of person. Always saw to it that I had a cup of tea or coffee before I left.'

'Have you seen her lately?'

'Who, Maree? No, but then I haven't been up there, you know, since Miss Stirling passed on.'

I was so staggered by the discovery that someone, apart from Albert, actually knew his wife's name that I temporarily ran out of questions and Mrs Chalmers glanced surreptitiously at her watch. Nipping in again at top speed, I said:

'Somebody told me they'd come to live round here. The house with the blue gate, I think they said.'

'Well, I never! I must keep a look out for her. To tell you the truth, I didn't even know they'd left the Rectory; but I suppose the old place will be sold up now. Sad to think of it, but you can't expect time to stand still. And it definitely won't for me. I must get along to the hospital now, or I'll have Matron on my tail. Sorry I can't be much help with the old wrist, but if I were you I'd exercise it as much as I could. Do pop in, though, any time you're this way, and let me know how it's getting on. I have enjoyed meeting you.'

She came out to the porch to see me off and I thanked her and apologised for taking up so much of her time, but she wasn't listening. She was looking away from me, down the road, and she said:

'It's funny you should mention Maree moving out here. The one with the blue gate is number six; I hadn't realised it. That's where Maureen lives.'

'Oh, are you sure? I didn't know she was a local girl. I thought Dr Macintosh got her through some agency in London.'

'So he may have done, but she's living here now. I ran into her the other morning, going in with a lot of parcels, and she told me she was sharing number six with three other girls from the hospital. There's quite a few houses round here are like that. People buy them up and put in a few sticks of furniture and let them to the nurses. Quite profitable, I shouldn't wonder, but the girls prefer it to being in the hostel, with all the rules and regulations. Well, I mustn't stop. Cheery bye for now, and do drop in again.'

'Successful morning?' Toby enquired, when I joined him in the summerhouse before lunch.

'One door shuts and the door of number six opens,' I informed him, sounding as cryptic as I could.

XVI

(i)

ON WEDNESDAY night Robin and the Chief Superintendent of Dedley C.I.D. made their arrest and by Thursday morning he was all set to shoot back to London. I agreed to go with him, since my appointment with Gerald Pettigrew had been fixed for the following day, but stipulated that we should both return on Friday evening, for Betsy's funeral. It was to be held at the Storhampton Parish Church one week to the day after her mother's.

Her death had been prominently featured in most of the papers, under headlines of which 'Third Death in Singer's Home' was a typical example, but there was no reference to accident or murder, so the police were presumably playing it very cagily.

She also got three paragraphs in the *Times* Obituary column, from which I was astounded to learn that she had achieved a brief operatic success, making her debut at the age of seven as the tot in *Madame Butterfly*. Evidently her voice had nowhere near approached Maudie's class, but she had trained under some distinguished teachers and had sung several minor rôles before her retirement in her early twenties. I assumed it was her marriage which had cut short this promising career, but when I consulted Toby on the subject he said it was a well-known fact that she had been sufficiently talented for Maud to become frenzied with jealousy and to use every stratagem at her command to undermine Betsy's confidence. However, as most of Toby's well-known facts were invented by himself on the spur of the moment, I did not take this as gospel.

Sophie had been cremated privately in London on Wednesday morning without fuss or publicity, and one way and another poor old Margot and Co. were going through a pretty bleak patch. I should have felt a lot worse about it than I did, had not some friend telephoned me within half an hour of my reaching Beacon Square to report that Piers had been seen at a first night with a very pretty girl in tow. He had been tight-lipped and preoccupied, making notes on his programme and giving it out that he was there at the behest of his editor, but the mask had slipped once or twice and, in the considered opinion of my informant, he was not absolutely inconsolable.

Betsy had once told me that if you were only to see Gerald when he was sitting down you would never guess there was anything wrong with him, but this was no longer true. He had undergone a shrinking process, as though the paralysis which afflicted his lower limbs were now encroaching on the rest of his muscles and he were succumbing to it without a struggle. His mouth twitched spasmodically and once or twice his hand embarrassed him by giving an involuntary jerk, but for the most part he was motionless in his wheelchair behind the desk, and the merry, seafaring eyes had grown glazed and dull, like those of a man already half dead.

'You'll appreciate,' he said, in a flat, formal voice, 'that the circumstances have changed since I asked you to come and see me.'

'I know and I half expected you to put me off. Since you didn't, I concluded there was some formality to be gone through in connection with Maud's bequest. However, as it now looks as though I won't be getting that, anyway . . .'

'Why do you say that?'

I explained briefly about the missing ring, though omitting any mention of Betsy's suspicions about the other jewellery, and he said:

'I'm sorry to hear that. I knew nothing about it. No doubt Betsy would have told me, but as you know I never saw her again after Maud's funeral. I'll have the matter taken up and we may be able to recover it for you, but

I'm passing all this business over to my partners. I don't feel equal to dealing with it myself any longer.'

'Well, for goodness sake don't go to any bother over the ring. That's the least of my worries.'

'In any case, it had nothing to do with my asking to see you. There was something else, which at the time I regarded as infinitely more pressing.'

'You mean, like Betsy's safety?'

A flicker of interest lightened his expression and for the first time he looked squarely back at me as he spoke.

'I had my eye on you, you know, when I was holding forth to them all about Maud's will, and it struck me then that you were probably the only one of the bunch who had genuine affection for Betsy and in whom she might be likely to confide. I can't say about Jasper. He may have been fond of her, in his own peculiar way, but he makes a fetish of callousness and he and I have nothing to say to each other. He would have been useless to me as an ally.'

'Will you tell me why you needed an ally and what you were afraid of?'

'Nothing specific. There was something in the wind I didn't altogether care for. I knew the will would be a shock, but Margot's reaction went beyond normal disappointment. There was vindictiveness in it. She has always been a jealous and possessive woman, you know, and she can be vindictive. Betsy is . . . was . . . about the most defenceless person who ever lived and I knew by all the signs that she was worried and nervous too. I was going to ask you to keep a watch out; stick as close as you could to her and report on any mischief Margot might be brewing.'

'What did you actually expect might happen?'

'Again, nothing specific. Nothing nearly so terrible as this. I had a hunch that Margot would go all out, by fair means or foul, to get her hands on the estate, but it didn't seriously enter my head that Betsy's life might be in danger.'

'Not even after that unfortunate accident of Sophie's?'

'But you must remember that I knew nothing about that until much later. Otherwise nothing would have induced me to go away and leave Betsy to the mercy of that crew. I'd have somehow got her to come up and stay with me in London for a while. Unhappily, no one thought of letting me know about the girl's death and I didn't get around to reading the newspapers until latish on Sunday. The truth is, I'm a useless old crock and the journey to Storhampton last Saturday knocked me up worse than usual. It was a strain all round.'

'But when you did read about Sophie, did you suspect that someone had killed her in mistake for Betsy?'

'I don't know that I took it as far as that, but it certainly increased my uneasiness. I had half a mind to drive back to Storhampton that evening but I wasn't in very good shape and anyway Betsy had an appointment here the following morning. Like a half-wit, I persuaded myself that this would take care of everything. I intended to put her on her guard, if I could, and persuade her to stay up in London. It wouldn't have been difficult, you know. She was such a good, selfless woman, I had only to drop a hint that I could do with a bit of looking after, and she'd have moved into my flat like a shot.'

I looked away and allowed my gaze to range round the soulless office, with its sombre furniture and forbidding-looking books, for Gerald had groped for his handkerchief and was making snorting noises into it. I wondered whether his home surroundings were equally cheerless and how much of the remaining brightness in his life had been extinguished with Betsy's death.

'Excuse me,' he said, putting the handkerchief away. 'Change in the weather. Caught a bit of a chill, I think. Did you say something?'

'Not aloud, but I had it in my mind to ask why you still wished to see me. It certainly wasn't to explain how it was that you were unable to prevent Betsy's death, because in the first place there was no need, and secondly you don't know me well enough to care what I think.'

'I do, as it happens. I told you just now that I'd had my eye on you and formed certain conclusions. I have to depend a good deal on first impressions nowadays. It's a trick, if you care to put it that way, which I've tried to cultivate. Being physically handicapped makes it essential to develop some other capacity above the norm, to even things up a bit. I won't bore you by telling you what my verdict on you added up to, but in this case it wasn't based solely on personal observation. My partner, who's quite a bright lad, got a similar impression when he saw you at Mrs Piers' inquest. He's a great cinema fan and he saw through your Mrs Price alias bang off. That's why he was at such pains to keep an eye on you during the proceedings.'

'Okay; so you guessed I was fond of Betsy and would be furious about her death, and you're right. Also you and your partner presumably came to the conclusion that I wasn't moronic, and I hope you're right there as well, but it still doesn't explain anything. It's even less credible that you invited me here in order to tell me how wonderful I was.'

'No, it was more by way of sounding you out, and I was pleased to hear you use the word "furious", instead of "shocked", or "saddened", because furious is how I feel too, among other things. If I had my own two legs I'd be after the brute who did it so fast you wouldn't see me for dust; but that's not on.'

'So you'd like me to go after him with my two legs instead?'

'Not quite, and I'm certainly not asking you to put yourself at risk. That would solve nothing and I might have even worse burdens on my conscience. What I'm going to ask you to take on is something in the way of a watching brief, without, if you can avoid it, giving these people a hint that you are observing them and listening for undercurrents in what they say.'

'And report back to you?'

'If anything turns up. Luckily, we have this matter of a missing ring to work on, so no eyebrows would be raised if you were to call here once in a while.'

'And what am I particularly to watch and listen for, Mr Pettigrew? I take it you have something or someone special in mind?'

'Yes,' he replied, 'you're right,' and then, to my profound astonishment, he added slowly, 'I'd like you to keep a look out for young Digby.'

'I must confess he's the last person I expected you to name.'

'Possibly, but I'm beginning to believe that one member of Betsy's family, if not two in collusion, must have been responsible for her death, and one has to start somewhere. Digby happens to be the only one who, from my personal knowledge, has something to explain.'

'Indeed? I suppose you can tell me what it is?'

'Yes, and I think you may not dismiss it as casually as the police so easily might. By itself, it's such a small thing but, as I say, one has to start somewhere. You may remember that I was the first of the party to return to the house after the funeral?'

'Yes, the others were all at the grave.'

'So we believed. In fact Digby was not.'

'How do you know?'

'I saw him as we drove in. Pete was going at a snail's pace, which is the way I like it, and I saw Digby come round the side of the house, between the house and the garage, that is; and what do you suppose he was carrying?'

'You really want me to guess?'

'Yes.'

'Well, I can't. Sorry to stumble at the first fence.'

'He was carrying a ladder.'

'Good God!'

'Naturally, it had no significance for me at the time. I was rather surprised to see him there, but I doubt if I'd have given it another thought if the silly boy hadn't gone out of his way to emphasise his presence. He must have seen my car but he pretended he hadn't. He dropped the ladder down by the side of the house, then turned and ambled back the way he had come. What do you make of that?'

'The only immediate thing that springs to mind is that it's a point in Albert's favour.'

'Explain, please!'

I gave him an account of Albert's abortive attempts to get into the bathroom where Betsy was already lying dead, and he said:

'Yes, I see. That does tie in, doesn't it? At the time, of course, my only reaction was a vague curiosity about what Digby was up to, and even that was temporarily submerged by the floods which Maud's will unleashed. It wasn't until I was driving past the same spot again, on my way out, that I recalled the incident and for some reason it seemed to crystallise the misgivings which had been building up all day. That was when I had the impulse to ask Pete to stop the car and give you a message. I can't say I'm often subject to premonitions; fairly unimaginative sort of chap, as a rule, but I'll go so far as to say that at that moment I experienced an almost physical sense of evil at work.'

'And how right you were! Thank you for telling me. I'll certainly keep my ear to the ground, and if anything does come up I'll let you know at once. Can I ask you one question before I go?'

'As many as you like.'

'Just one. If you won't think it impertinent, could you tell me about Betsy's will? I mean, who gets the money now?'

'You may find the answer somewhat ironical. You'll realise of course that her will as not been changed since she inherited her mother's estate. We can't tell how she would have disposed of things, had there been time, but as it stands, all property, investments and other holdings pass to Jasper.'

'Ah!'

'Yes, but this is the curious part; the jewellery is bequeathed to Margot. When the will was drawn up Jasper stood to inherit something like ten or twelve thousand pounds. Even allowing for the double death duties, his share will total almost ten times that amount. Margot's position is even more startling in a way. Instead of the few trinkets she would have received if Betsy had died a week earlier, she now gets the whole of Maudie's collection as well. I can't be precise about the value because the market varies, but most of it is really big stuff, which she acquired or had thrust upon her in her heyday. I can tell you this much, however; there's a tiara and matching diamond necklace which alone are insured for around forty thousand pounds.'

'So we're back where we came in, with all the old faces squarely in the picture again,' I told Robin, while discussing these matters as we drove out of London on Friday evening. 'With the possible exception of Dickie and Jasper.'

'I don't quite go along with that. Dickie may be presumed to benefit where Margot does, and Jasper certainly isn't doing too badly.'

'Yes, but only because things took the wrong turn at the beginning. If Betsy had drunk the milk instead of Maud, Jasper would have been out in the cold with a measly ten thousand. What's more, once Maud was dead, he had only to tell Betsy to hand everything over to him and she'd have done it in a flash. If it had ever come to a tussle between him and Margot he'd have won hands down. He was the last person who needed to kill her to get possession of it.'

'What construction do you put on Gerald's story about Digby?'

'God knows, Robin, although it ties in with his car being missing at that particular time. Presumably he drove it away and parked it somewhere out of sight of the house; and then if anyone had noticed his absence he could say that he felt so broken up by the loss of his old gran that he couldn't face the funeral and had gone for a spin in the country; something like that.'

'He'd have had a job hiding the car, wouldn't he? It's fairly conspicuous and, if it had come to the crunch, the chances are that someone, somewhere would have noticed it standing empty.'

'Yes, but he's such an ass that he may not have thought of that. Or perhaps he only meant to fall back on that story as a last resort, hoping to get away with the tale about having come in late and sat at the back of the Church, which in fact he did get away with.'

'All the same, he'd have to have taken the car some distance away and it wouldn't have left him much time for returning on foot and carving up the balcony posts before Gerald arrived on the scene. And that's not all, Tessa. Wouldn't there have been a gigantic risk of you or Betsy catching him in the act?'

'Not really. It's true that we were in the morning room at the time, but well away from the window, and anyway he'd have been fairly safe so long as he'd propped the ladder up between Betsy's balcony and the one leading out of Maud's room. All the same, I don't seriously suspect Digby of having a hand in that job.'

'Because of your theory that it was done some days earlier?'

'Oh no,' I said, wondering vaguely what could have given him that idea, 'not at all. It's simply that there was one very subtle touch about Sophie's fall, which I couldn't mention before because Betsy had seen fit to remove the evidence.'

'What evidence?'

'Well, actually, Robin, it was Margot's hat.'

'Margot's hat?' he repeated in a dazed tone. 'Whatever next?'

'You wouldn't be so surprised if you'd seen it as I did, lying on the ground beside Sophie. It gave me a proper jolt, I can tell you, because just for a moment I thought she must have been holding one of the cats when she fell. That's exactly what it looked like; a dead cat. But I don't think it came down with Sophie and I'm sure it didn't get there by accident. I think Betsy saw the point of it long before I did, and that's why she threw it back into the house even before I went to telephone Dr Macintosh.'

'And what was the point of it?'

'Well, look at it this way, Robin: on the face of it, there was something so hit and miss about that balcony trap. It must have been planned for Betsy, but days or weeks might have gone by before she fell into it. Perhaps the murderer wasn't in any special hurry when he set it up, but then he realised that she would soon be moving out of that room and back to the Stables, so he had to act quickly. Hence Margot's hat.'

'Meaning that Betsy, seeing it from above, would mistake it for a dead cat and lean over the balcony to get a closer view?'

'Yes, and that's precisely what she would have done, don't you think? And that, I imagine, is just what Sophie did. You may remember that she had this special kind of affinity with cats? Some people might have ignored it, but she wasn't one of them, and neither was Betsy. And that's really why I rule out Digby. He simply hasn't got the sort of mind to invent a trick like that.'

'You can't tell. He may not express himself very lucidly, but that could be because his thought processes are more complicated than the average, not less; or even that they've become so, simply because he finds it hard to communicate.'

'Well, that's a novel idea, Robin. Is it based on experience?'

'Not entirely. I simply feel it's a mistake to assume that inarticulate people are necessarily simple minded. It's sometimes the other way round. Take Toby, for example.'

'He's not what I call inarticulate.'

'No, perhaps laconic is more the word for him, but certainly a good deal less chatty than, say, Lulu.'

'Who's not very bright, I agree; although they make a good team. It was a remark Toby made about Lulu which first gave me the idea that we were wrong in thinking that Sophie had been enticed on to the balcony and then pushed. In other words, that the murderer, having laid his bait, wasn't necessarily anywhere near her when she fell. Toby said that even Lulu wouldn't be silly enough to fall off a balcony, however keen she might be to see what was down below. I suddenly visualised it from that angle, instead of the other way on, and I realised the significance of Margot's hat.'

'Well, I don't think we can give her much credit for that.'

'Maybe not, but later on she produced another valuable item, right off her own bat. She told me that the Family Planners met on Tuesday, not Wednesday. And she was right, you know, Robin. I checked up on the Town Hall notice board when I was there for Sophie's inquest. So why did Betsy pretend to have been at the meeting on the day Maud died, which was also by a curious coincidence the day Gerald brought the new will down for her to sign?'

'I take this to be a rhetorical question to which you will now provide the answer?'

'No such luck. I hoped you might.'

'Perhaps what you need is another chat with Lulu.'

'And perhaps what I need even more is for you to have an unofficial chat with Chief Inspector Mackenzie.'

'I can do better than that. I'm down for an official chat with him in his office tomorrow morning.'

'Honestly, Robin, you might have told me!'

'It was practically inevitable, don't you think? With the Dedley case wrapped up and on its way to the post, who more obvious than I to answer the Storhampton call?'

'Although, if you had told me, I am not sure I would have been so free in passing on everything Gerald said. On the other hand, he didn't swear me to secrecy.'

'And since his object is to catch the villain, why should he quarrel with the methods?'

'Quite so, my love. And with your expertise, Mackenzie's resources and my inside information all working to the same goal, I don't see there can be much to stop us, do you?'

'I wish I shared your confidence,' he replied, changing into low gear for the long, winding climb up to Roakes Common. 'I have my own ideas about who's responsible, but I very much doubt if it will ever be proven.'

As it happened, I also had some ideas on the subject, and furthermore had already begun to work out a few plans to find the proof. Vanity urged my getting to it ahead of Chief Inspector Mackenzie, but I was not above seeking help from the rival firm and I asked Robin if he would use his official status to dig up a piece of information for me.

'I might,' he replied warily. 'Depends what you want to know.'

'It's a question of property,' I explained. 'The owner-ship of certain property, to be precise. I could probably get it for myself, given time, but it might take days; whereas Mackenzie would probably only need to lift the telephone.'

'Tell me exactly what you want to know,' Robin said, and I did so.

XVII

(i)

ROBIN had taken the car, to keep his appointment with Chief Inspector Mackenzie and Toby was loth, if that's not too weak a word, to lend me the Mercedes; so I had to hire a taxi to take me down to Storhampton.

Owen, the driver, was an old friend, dating back to my spinster days, and as we had a gap of several months to fill in our exchange of family news, almost half the distance had been covered before we broached the subject of my immediate destination. Owen was ablaze with curiosity to learn that I was on my way to the Rectory for Betsy's funeral, although casting a somewhat disapproving look at my outfit. The hot weather had returned, not quite on the scale of its former tropical splendour, but promising enough to enable me to wear my newest summer dress, which happened to be bright yellow.

'It's all right,' I explained. 'I have it on the best authority that Mrs Craig specifically asked for no mourning.'

'Ah,' he said sombrely, as though I had confirmed some dark suspicion of his own. 'Yes, I daresay she did. Said a lot of funny things, I shouldn't wonder.'

'What can you mean, Owen? She was vague and absentminded sometimes, but not in the least off her head.'

'Well, I don't know what else you'd call it. Kindest thing, I'd say, and I wouldn't be the one to cast the first stone. She had her troubles, we all know that, and I dare-say the old lady's death was the last straw.'

I was so flabbergasted by these remarks that it took me a minute or two to find the right words to protest.

'Oh, come on, Owen! You're surely to God not hinting that Mrs Craig took her own life?'

It was his turn to become speechless and he went brick red, glaring ahead of him and pressing his foot down a little too hard on the accelerator. This turned out rather badly because, as we swept round a downhill bend, we ran smack into a herd of cows lolloping across the road. He had to stand on the brake and come to a dead stop while they banged up against the bonnet, staring in at us through the windscreen with moody expressions and indolently flapping their tails against the side windows.

'Is that really what you meant?' I asked.

'Sorry to speak out of turn,' he mumbled. 'But I took it for granted you knew.'

'But it isn't true, Owen.'

'It's what everybody hereabouts is saying,' he replied obstinately; then, finding a new outlet for his annoyance, began to abuse the farmer for cluttering up the highway with his stupid animals.

'It's all right,' I said. 'We haven't got to catch a train.'

'All right for some.'

This was true in a way, because personally I had begun to feel grateful for the interlude which was giving me time to reconsider my attitude. I now saw the error of persisting in my denials as to the cause of Betsy's death, for it was quite possible that the police had reasons of their own for encouraging if not instigating the rumour that it was suicide.

His brief outburst concluded, Owen also started to relax and, as the car groped forward again past the receding sea of black and white rumps, he pulled out a pack of cigarettes and offered it to me before taking one himself.

'Do you know anyone called Ted Williams?' I asked, fishing for my lighter.

'I used to know a bookie by that name.'

'This one's a tobacconist.'

'Oh, him! You mean the chap as had the shop up near the hospital?'

'That's the one.'

'Can't say I knew him exactly. I used to go in there sometimes, when I had a long wait, but not more than I could help. It was a run-down sort of place and he always seemed to be out of the brands I smoke. He's gone now.'

'So I heard. Has he retired?'

'Doubt it. There was some tale about his old man dying and he had to take care of his mother, but it's more likely he'd done a bunk, I'd say. Left a good many debts behind, so they tell me.'

'Married?'

'Not that I know of. If he was, he didn't have his missus serving in the shop, and she certainly didn't do much cleaning up after hours. What's it to you?'

'Someone I know is thinking of taking over the shop and modernising it a bit.'

'It's a good site,' he admitted. 'There's nowhere else up there when the pubs are shut and there's some people can't wait to jet their fingers round a fag when they've been hanging about in the Out-Patients half the day. Do you mind if I drop you off at the gate instead of going right up? I've got to collect the old lady from Ballards Farm next and drive her over to Reading. She's on the fussy side and those blasted cows have made me a bit late.'

'You can drop me where you like, but you'll have to go into the drive to turn round, won't you?'

'No, I won't. There's a right of way through the woods I can take, just opposite the Rectory.'

'I thought that was just a bridle path?'

'Used to be. They've widened it now, so as the tractors can get through when they're cutting timber. It's not much of a surface, but all right in this weather and it brings me out just where I want to be.'

'Okay, Owen, let me out here, then; and thanks a lot.'

'Cheerioh! Mind how you go!'

One way and another, a rewarding twenty minutes on several counts, and I was inclined to feel, as I trudged up the drive, that the chief inspector would be well advised to start buckling on his roller skates.

(ii)

The front door was wide open, as usual, and, coming from the midday glare outside, it took a second or two to adjust my sight to the shadowy interior. When the picture cleared I saw that its central feature was a composition in black and white, represented by two figures posed against the staircase. One of them was Piers, in a dark suit, standing with his back to me and talking to Albert, who faced him and was therefore the first to notice my arrival. He appeared to have lost about a stone in weight and his white jacket sagged over rounded shoulders and drooped to a limp, uneven hemline just above his knees.

One hand gripped the banister knob, but he half raised the other, either in a feeble salute or as a warning to his companion, and Piers spun round and came towards me, all smiles.

He not only wore a dark suit but a black tie as well, although I reminded myself that he was probably in mourning for Sophie, which would naturally take precedence over Betsy's wishes, and the effect was certainly becoming to his flaxen beauty.

'Why, Tessa my darling, how good of you to come,' he said, linking his arm in mine and kissing the top of my head.

'I wanted to. You know how I felt about Betsy.'

'Yes, indeed, and she was utterly devoted to you. We all know that, my dearest. Oh goodness, how terrible it all is! One misses her desperately. My poor mother is just about on her knees. I was giving Albert a few instructions about lunch and so on, since no one else seems inclined to lift a finger.'

'Poor Albert, he looks simply terrible.'

'And feels it, my darling, as much as any of us, I do believe. I begged him to come and sit with us all in Church, but he absolutely won't. He means to go down there later, on his own.'

There was something so grotesquely familiar in these remarks that I was mentally transported back to this very day, exactly a week ago, when Betsy had used almost the identical words. So when Piers said: 'Oh, do let us stroll outside for a bit, away from this ghastly, oppressive house,' I found myself being led back through the front door as though in a dream.

'That's better,' he said, his arm still clutching mine. 'One can breathe out here, and there's something I want to ask you. Personally I never intend to set foot in that repulsive old mausoleum after today. I do hope some nasty little speculator will come along very quickly and offer Jasper huge sums, so that we can forget all about it.'

'I should imagine Jasper feels the same, and luckily he has no need to hang on for a good price.'

'How very true! It's such a tonic talking to you, Tessa dear. Both those dainty feet so firmly planted on the ground, it fairly bucks one up. And I do appreciate your coming today, I honestly do, my darling. It's really quite brave of you.'

'No worse for me than the rest of you.'

'Ah, but we had no choice, had we? Whereas you could so easily have backed out. Not everyone would be so trusting as to visit a house where three violent deaths had occurred in a single week.'

'Three? Do you include your grandmother?'

He broke into a nervous titter and simultaneously his arm went taut and he drew my own closer to his side, so that I felt I were being pinioned by a steel rod.

'Don't be so literal, Tessa.'

'All right, but what was it you wanted to ask me?'

'An indescribably small thing, my darling, so very trivial; but you were on rather special terms with Betsy, weren't you? I mean, she used to confide in you?'

'Not me specially.'

'Oh, come on, now! I've heard her yattering away to you for hours on end.'

'Only because I listened.'

'Oh, we are being difficult, aren't we? But that's exactly what I mean. Did you ever hear her say anything about some recording tapes?'

I had been expecting something like this and, although I had the answer ready, was careful not to jump in with it too quickly.

'Recording tapes?' I repeated in a musing voice. 'No, I don't think so. Not that I recall.'

'Well, think again, there's a good girl.'

'Why? Is it important?'

'Not particularly, my heart. I've already told you that. It's simply that my potty old grandma did see fit to appoint me her official biographer and I might as well salvage that much from the wreck.'

'And these tapes are missing, is that it?'

'Oh, you are such a clever baby! How do you manage it?'

'Sarcasm will get you nowhere,' I informed him.

We had been walking quite slowly, but always further away from the house and had now reached the shrubbery which bordered that section of the lawn. Piers stopped and looked down at me.

'You're a dark horse sometimes, aren't you, Tessa? I wish I could make up my mind about you.'

'I doubt if it would do you much good. However, I'll let you know if I do remember anything.'

'Oh, forget it,' he said impatiently, starting to walk back the way we had come and slightly relaxing his grip on my arm. 'It was just a thought. Minimal importance.'

'Except that these tapes might contain valuable material for your book?'

'I doubt it. The old person was pretty past it; rambling on in a stream of unconsciousness, most of the time. All the same, one wouldn't necessarily want any unauthorised person to get hold of them. Rather too many sharks about in this world, you know.'

'Yes, I've noticed it.'

'They'll turn up, I daresay. Where's Robin, by the way? You don't tell me he's left you to face this ordeal on your own?'

'No, he'll be along presently. He had some business to see to first.'

'Business?' he repeated sharply. 'I thought he was in the police?'

'Yes, he is. Don't be so literal, Piers,' I mocked.

As though a switch had been pulled, releasing a torrent of dammed up irritation, he dropped my arm and in the same movement clapped his palm against the nape of my neck, then thrust my head down, squeezing his fingers and thumb into the flesh under my jawbone, and pushed me forward at a brisk pace.

For all I know, he would have marched me the whole way back to the house in this fashion, but luckily I was spared the discomfort and indignity of it by the arrival of Robin, who came swooping into the drive like the goodie in the last reel. He made a half circle and came to rest by the edge of the lawn about twenty yards away from us, and Piers, who had withdrawn his hand with the speed of a conjuror, darted forward to greet him.

'I'd have been here sooner,' Robin explained, 'only I had a puncture. Just outside in the lane, fortunately. Hop in, Tessa, and you can guide me to that pet garage of yours. I'd like to get the tyre repaired before we have to drive back to London.'

'Oh, come in and have a drink first, my dear,' Piers begged him. 'You've got time.'

'No thanks, I'd rather get to a garage before all the mechanics knock off for the weekend.'

'But there's no need for you to go. Come inside and have a drink and we'll get Digby to take it for you.'

'I can't imagine why he would want to do that.'

'He will if I tell him to,' Piers replied simply.

'Did you really have a flat tyre?' I asked, as we drove off.

'Of course not. It was the only excuse I could think of. I wanted to get you on your own for a minute and warn you about wandering off with strange men and allowing them to strangle you.'

'Oh, you noticed that, did you? You can turn off into the trees here, if you want to park out of sight. There's a through-way, so it's perfectly legal. Yes, in some respects, Piers is very strange indeed; but I got entangled in that little scene through sheer inattention. I'll be on my guard now and it won't happen again.'

'That's a relief. I got your item of information, by the way. You were quite right. He owns that house and three others in the same neighbourhood.'

'Splendid! And I must say, Robin, it was decent of that sour old Mackenzie to jump to it so quickly.'

'He was rather tickled. You've got him all wrong, you know, Tessa. That patronising manner is just good, honest, old-fashioned gaucherie. He's rather impressed by you, as it happens; told me you'd been extremely helpful. I think he'd be ready to take you on, if you ever felt like changing your career and becoming a W.P.C.'

'He'll make me an honorary superintendent,' I said, 'when he hears what else I've got for him.'

XVIII

(i)

I CANNOT tell how Betsy's funeral compared with Maud's, but it was short, dignified and very moving. I was obliged to keep my dark glasses on all the way through, and even the hard faced Margot had to mop up once or twice.

Jasper was present, still in his sloppy, canvas shoes and looking more sulky than sorrowful, but he sat well away from the rest of the family, who occupied the front pew. They were joined at the last minute by a very pretty, tall girl of about twenty-five, who was a stranger to me. She hesitated beside their pew and was turning away to a seat across the aisle when Dickie, who was nearest to her, moved down a place and made room for her between himself and Piers.

Chief Inspector Mackenzie also came in late and stationed himself at the back. He and Robin ostentatiously cut each other dead, which was no doubt in accordance with the prepared script, and the young man who had been at the inquest once again represented Pettigrew and Barrett. He attached himself to me, as we returned in the slow procession to the house, with Piers and Margot at its head.

I asked after Gerald and he said: 'Dodgy, you know. He lives on his nerves a good deal, I think.'

'And when they collapse, there's nothing much left?'

'That's about it.'

'Except for Pete, of course, the man who looks after him?'

'Oh yes, old Pete. A trifle boneheaded, but dependable as they come. I say, are you working on anything at the moment? I loved your last one.'

I thanked him and we had a brief though enjoyable chat about developments in this field, in the course of which Robin unobtrusively fell a few paces behind, as befitted a husband who had heard it all before, and when I glanced back I saw that he had teamed up with Digby.

We had got to within a few yards of the front door when my solicitor friend changed the subject.

'You'll be getting a letter about this in a few days, but I've already mentioned it to Mrs Roche and I thought you might like to know that Mrs Craig had remembered you in her will.'

'Oh dear!' I said, stopping in my tracks and automatically rummaging for the sunglasses, until I remembered I still had them on, 'I mean, how very kind of her!'

'She's left you her pearl necklace. Do you know it?'

'I've seen her wear it once or twice. It was her mother's wedding present, I believe.'

'You don't sound too happy about it.'

'I'm grateful, naturally. It's just that people always seem to be leaving me their pet pieces of jewellery and, so far, I can't say that much good has come of it.'

'Oh yes, Miss Stirling's ring. That was rotten luck, I agree, but there's quite a good chance that the police will be able to trace it. Anyway, cheer up! There's no reason to suppose that the pearls will cause you any trouble.'

Robin rejoined us at this point and the young man continued on into the house. I never saw him again after that day, so cannot tell whether he makes a habit of throwing out such false predictions, or whether this was the exception.

'We don't have to stay long, do we?' Robin muttered, as we entered the cavernous gloom. 'I mean, I could do with a drink, but preferably not here. If you took those glasses off you might be able to see something.'

'Only ten minutes. Perhaps we ought just to say good-bye to Margot. It might look rude to leave without a word.'

The word with Jasper came first, however. He was slumped in an armchair, with a tumblerful of whisky in his hand, and he stuck out a foot to bar my way, or to trip me up, for all I know.

'You here again?' he enquired.

'We're going in a minute, you'll be relieved to hear.'

'I wish to God they'd all go,' he said, glaring morosely at his assembled relatives. They were grouped in a tight bunch as usual, although one member short, Digby having done one of his vanishing acts.

'Occasions of this kind get on my nerves,' Jasper explained.

I forbore to point out that it was not one which was likely to be repeated many times in his life, because it was evident that he was far from sober and that very little would be needed to exacerbate that sensitive spirit. Choosing a safer subject, I asked him about the girl who had come late to the church. I had noticed that she was still among us and was at that moment talking to a besotted-looking Dickie, giving him the full treatment with seductive smiles and adoring looks.

'Who are you talking about? You do ask such a lot of bloody questions always. Oh, her! Don't you know? She's one of the nurses. Maureen something or other. I haven't the faintest idea what she's doing here. If you want it straight and unadulterated, Miss Quizzy Crichton, I don't know what any of this crew is doing here. They didn't give a damn for Betsy, as you bloody well know, and I wish to God they'd all go home and leave me in peace.'

The spectacle of Jasper loudly parading his emotions had become so familiar that it was easy to overlook the fact that some of them might be genuine, but for once I found myself pitying him. Although his speech was slurred, there was no mistaking the wretchedness in it, and his expression as he looked across the hall to where Margot and the others were gathered, had lost all its insolent cockiness.

'I'm sorry, Jasper. I understand how you must be feeling, but we really are leaving now. I'll say goodbye to Margot and then we'll be off. With any luck, it could start a general move. Ring me up in London, if there's anything I can do.'

He nodded, before taking another hefty swig at his drink, and I moved away.

'Goodbye, Margot.'

'Going already? Well, we shall be, too, as soon as Digby has finished loading up the car. We used to leave a few spare macs and boots down here, but I don't imagine we'll be needing them in future. It was good of you to come. Betsy left you her pearl necklace. Did they tell you?'

'Yes, I hope you don't mind?'

'Not in the least, my dear. It's quite a pretty little thing, I should think it would suit you. I asked Jasper to get it out for you to see, but needless to say he hasn't the faintest idea where she kept it. He thought Albert might know.'

'Oh, it doesn't matter. I am sure Albert has a lot more important things to see to.'

'You'd think so, wouldn't you, my dear? But Jasper calmly informed me that he'd given him the rest of the day off, as it wouldn't hurt us all to fend for ourselves for once. Isn't that charming? You'd have thought he might at least have had the tact to wait until after the funeral before telling me, in so many words, that he is now master of the house and I should mind my own business.'

'Well, I don't know, Margot. Albert's been through a gruelling time, and you must admit it's exactly what Betsy would have done.'

'That's beside the point. However, you want to be off, so I mustn't keep you. Come and see me in Lowndes Square one day,' she added, not meaning it.

'I'll do that,' I assented fervently, not meaning it either.

The boot of Margot's car was open and Digby had his head inside. He did not take it out when we called good-bye to him.

'I have a strong sensation of anti-climax,' I told Robin, as he started the car. 'Of something lacking.'

'So have I,' he admitted. 'Though luckily I know just where to find it. What's that place called overlooking the river? The Angel?'

'No, the Saracen.'

'That's the one.'

'I was expecting something to happen,' I explained, still harping on the same theme, after we were installed on a bench in the window. 'A sort of Catharsis, if that's the right word.'

'How can I tell if it's the right word until I know what you mean by it?'

'A bust up, that's what I mean. I expected the murderer to show his hand in some way, so that you would dash forward and foil his wicked plot and Mackenzie would pounce out of the bushes and apprehend him. I don't know why I expected something like that to happen. At least, I do, as a matter of fact.'

'Well, which?'

'I had this fixed idea that something still remains to be done and that whatever it is would have to be done while we were all there in the house; and yet no one made a move.'

'You still haven't made it clear why you expected anyone would.'

'Not from choice, necessarily, but something tells me this business isn't finished yet. There's a loose end to be tied up, and today was the last chance.'

'Perhaps you'd like to go back? You could always do your celebrated act of having mislaid your glasses. He or she may just have been waiting until we were safely off the premises.'

'No, it can't be that. Margot told me she was leaving almost immediately, and where she goes her little flock is bound to follow. But it doesn't add up. You see, Robin, there's been a kind of crazy pattern linking all these crimes. They were so haphazard in one way, more like lethal booby traps, and the murderer appears to have been pretty casual about who got caught in them; but they had two things in common. They could all have been set up by any one of them, and also aimed at any one of them. That can't happen any more, because it's highly improbable that any of Margot's bunch will ever come back.'

'The trouble with you, Tessa, is that you expect everyone, murderers included, to behave exactly on the lines you've laid down for them, and it doesn't always work out. Drink up and relax; and for heaven's sake let's talk of something else.'

I endeavoured to follow this advice, but my efforts were not exactly crowned with success.

'You didn't get anywhere with Digby, I suppose?' I asked, after a long pause.

'No, there wasn't time; but he was certainly fidgety and he bolted like a rabbit as soon as we were indoors. Not that that means anything. Probably his normal reactions when addressed by one of the fascist pigs. Also I don't call that changing the subject.'

'I apologise,' I said, setting my glass down. 'It's anti-social of me, I realise that, but I feel so uneasy. There's something missing, I know there is, and I shan't sleep a wink until I find it.'

(ii)

The missing piece turned up in the nick of time and, not surprisingly, Lulu was the one to supply it.

Refusing, as she put it, to take no for an answer, she had bidden us to drinkies at White Gables on Saturday evening. Fortified by the news, just received, of Ellen's imminent return from Tunisia, and aware that the summer house was a little too cramped to accommodate all three of us for an entire evening, Toby had capitulated. Seven o'clock, therefore, found us seated in the cosiest sitting-room imaginable and surrounded on all sides by rubbery coasters shaped like ivy leaves.

In other respects, the pattern was much as before. Robin and Toby promptly segregated themselves on one side of the room, leaving Lulu to me on the other. Once more she assured me of her pleasure in my company and of her instinctive feeling that we had so much in common, while regularly reprimanding the other two for trying to listen in.

She began by asking me about Ellen and her expression clouded a little on learning that the Tunisian interlude was nearly over. To divert her mind from this sad prospect, I asked about her own experiences of foreign travel and was rewarded with a lengthy dissertation on a Mediterranean cruise which she and her hubby had taken the year before he died, in which they had met up with a jolly crowd and had no end of larks, including getting up a theatrical entertainment for the other passengers, which had drawn the personal compliments of the captain.

So it came almost as a relief when she offered to show me round the house, with a view to pointing out the various improvements she had made, and when Robin and Toby had been loudly forbidden to accompany us and complied with who knew what reluctance, we set off on our tour.

As it happened, I had only seen one or two of the downstairs rooms during the Griswold era, so the interest in Lulu's innovations was not overpowering, although I was able to assure her with total sincerity that they would have earned the unqualified approval of Sylvia. However, there was one new addition which inspired ungrudging admiration and this was an extra bathroom which had been converted out of one of the larger bedrooms. It was a positive palace of a bathroom, fitted with every plumbing gadget known to man, and I stood lost in wonder while she expatiated on the dimensions of the bath, drew my attention to the thick pile carpet, which was guaranteed splash-proof, and slid back one after another of the cupboard doors to reveal the richness of sheets and bath towels within.

This being the climax of the expedition, we then returned to the drawing-room, where Toby instantly rose to his feet, saying that Mrs Parkes became very touchy if the dinner was kept waiting. It was only a half truth because Mrs Parkes also became very touchy if the dinner was not kept waiting, but it served its purpose and we got away after only five minutes of argument.

Lying in bed a few hours later and unable to sleep because of the conglomeration of thoughts and memories, I found the process of tidying them up being constantly interfered with by images of poor Lulu in her hopeless quest to make a hubby out of Toby. Scraps of her conversation kept inserting themselves between me and the main theme until I finally gave up and took myself, step by step and word by word, through the forty minutes we had spent in her house, in order to expunge them conclusively. In doing so, I naturally fell asleep.

There followed dreams of terrifying and chaotic order, and at one moment, against all the advice of the shadowy characters in the background, I was decking myself out in a tiara, to go on a picnic; but then suddenly I was in Lulu's bathroom, being sucked down by her splashproof carpet, which had turned into green quicksand. They had all gone to the picnic without me and I woke up yelling. Instantly a shutter clicked in my brain and the picture cleared. So I went on yelling until I had woken Robin as well.

'You've got to get up,' I said. 'Now, this minute. It's terribly urgent. Please, Robin, do as I say. I'll explain afterwards.'

'Okay, okay, but where's the fire?'

'At the Rectory. Go down and telephone Mackenzie. Tell him to meet us there as quick as he can. They'll part with his home number if you do it.'

To my intense relief and gratitude, he did not argue, but pulled on a dressing-gown and blearily groped under the bed for his slippers.

'Oh, and Robin,' I called out, as he shuffled to the door, 'tell him to bring his best safe-blower and lock-picker with him.'

He asked no questions and twenty minutes later I was blinded by the glare of headlights as he brought the car up to the gate. On the way down to Storhampton I told him what I expected to find.

They had to break the door down because, after several abortive attempts, D.C. Ramsay admitted defeat, complaining that this particular lock had that little bit extra.

'It's a special one which the insurance company forced on them,' I explained to Robin. 'They used to keep the key on that ledge above the door, which rather defeated the object, but naturally it's not there now.'

'Stand back, please!' Mackenzie warned, doing so himself, as two of his henchmen went into action.

When they had smashed the lock they pulled the door outwards, which was just as well because Albert was lying with his head against it, and what little life remained to him would certainly have been snuffed out if it had collapsed on top of him. As it was, he was unconscious, but still breathing. At one point, he must have clawed at the shelves, in his despairing fight against suffocation, for some sheets and pillowcases had slid out and were tumbled about his legs.

They dragged him on to the landing and I peered into the dark interior and saw that the safe door was open. Then Robin went downstairs to telephone for an ambulance, while Mackenzie rasped out some instructions and set the wheels in motion for the pouncing and apprehending part.

XIX

'HE WAS a strange man, all right,' I remarked. 'And never more so than yesterday, at Betsy's funeral. That was the first time I'd seen the mood turn violent.'

We were driving up the M4 as I spoke, all three of us in the front seat of Toby's Mercedes, having formed ourselves into a welcoming committee for Ellen.

'Violent?' Toby repeated. 'Nobody told me that. In what way?'

'It was half jokey, but there was an underlying violence. I am sorry to keep repeating it, but it is the only word. I think he had begun to see me as a threat and in some corner of his black heart he really wanted to kill me.'

'And yet, so far as he was aware, you'd done nothing to arouse such wild passions?'

'I know, Toby, but he always reacted instinctively, at any rate where women were concerned. He was so good-looking and attractive, when he set out to be, and he went through life using women to get exactly what he wanted, until I suppose he began to feel he had such power over them that he could literally get away with murder. It must have been a ghastly shock when things began to go wrong, and perhaps he associated me with it in some way; but of course the real trouble was that the one for whom the whole plot had been devised was so obviously casting her net elsewhere.'

Robin had been silent for several minutes, but, corresponding with this, I had become conscious of a sensation of overcrowding on my left, as though he had literally swelled up by several pounds since leaving the house, and he now burst out:

'Can we be speaking of the same man? What's all this about wanting to kill you and being so attractive? It's the first I've heard of it.'

'But he was, you know, Robin. Men could never see it, but women fell for him in vanloads, even tough old Maud. And, before you tell me she was in her dotage, how about Maureen? She was dishy enough, by anyone's standards.'

'I'll have to take your word for it. Personally, I always found him a conceited bore, and stupid with it. And when did he try to kill you, I should like to know?'

'I didn't say that exactly, but I swear there was a latent murderous instinct at work. He stuck his leg out and tried to trip me up. I don't pretend for a moment that it would have been curtains if I'd fallen, or even that he had that consciously in mind, but I was wearing dark glasses and I could have come one hell of a cropper on that stone floor.' Toby said: 'Perhaps we should be charitable and write it off as nervous tension. I suppose Albert was already in the linen cupboard by this time, which must have been quite a worry.'

'Yes, he was. Margot had spoken to Jasper about the pearl necklace before Betsy's funeral, and he must have seen his chance. He pretended to be completely indifferent about it, but in fact he asked Albert right away to go and fetch it. Then he followed him upstairs, in his sneakers, and as soon as Albert had his back turned and was fiddling with the safe, he slammed the door on him, afterwards putting it about that he'd given him the day off.'

'Very cool,' Toby said. 'Is this where we turn off, or the next one?'

'The next one. We're still in Slough, believe it or not. Yes, it was cool, but you could tell he was a bag of nerves underneath. Luckily for him the Rectory had been constructed as a Victorian version of a medieval fortress, but still he must have been scared stiff that someone would hear Albert banging and shouting, even through those solid old walls. He couldn't wait for everyone to go, and the situation was made quite intolerable by the fact that Maureen was flashing her eyes at everyone but him. That could have been an act, but she looked to me like someone who goes around collecting scalps, and I bet she's now ditched old Jasper, hasn't she?'

'Yes. She admits to collaborating with him, but she insists that the milk only contained some perfectly harmless sedative. She maintains that the purpose of it, so far as she knew, was simply to ensure that Betsy fell into a deep enough sleep to enable her to desert her post for a couple of hours and visit Jasper at the Stables. Nothing will shake her on that, and I think she may well get away with it. Jasper will carry the can.'

'It's maddening really, Robin, because although she may not have committed any crime, I'll bet you anything she put him up to it. She was an essential cog and she must have realised what the plan was.'

'Which is more than I do,' Toby said, pulling over into the slow lane, as the airport sign loomed up on our left. 'Are we now saying that the milk was supposed to finish off Maudie, after all?'

'Certainly we are. It's highly unlikely that the dose was strong enough to kill Betsy. In fact, the last thing they wanted was for her to die first. Maureen's job was to throw some extra salt into the soup on Maud's dinner tray, not enough to put her off completely, just to bring on a raging thirst an hour or two later, and then beat it over to the Stables. Of course she'd now deny all the bit about the salt, but Betsy mentioned it right at the beginning. They ran the slight risk that if Dr Macintosh had found out that Maureen had abandoned his patient he'd have fired her on the spot, but Betsy was the last person to raise a rumpus of that kind. In fact, she secretly welcomed the chance to wait on Maud herself.'

'It was a neat plan,' Robin admitted, 'because if Maud's death had been investigated, all the evidence would have pointed to the milk being intended for Betsy. It wouldn't have done her any permanent harm if she'd drunk it, and furthermore Jasper hadn't the shred of a motive for murdering her. She not only allowed him perfect freedom to go his own way, but she was a comparatively poor woman at that time.'

'Where I made my mistake,' I confessed, 'was in insisting that he still had no motive when she became a rich one. We all knew that Jasper had only to ask and she would have handed over the lot.'

'But you had reckoned without Maureen?'

We were grinding through the Heathrow tunnel as Toby spoke, and his voice came out in a muffled roar.

'Too true,' I yelled back, then dropped my voice by a few hundred decibels as we shot into the sunlight again. 'Maureen was out for wedding bells, and even Betsy might have jibbed at handing out a quarter of a million with one hand and divorce papers with the other. She closed her eyes to a hell of a lot where Jasper was concerned, but losing him was the one thing she wouldn't tolerate.'

'And where did Digby's little jape fit into all this, I wonder? By the way, which building are we supposed to go to? Did anyone remember to find out?'

'Tunisia is in Africa,' Robin told him. 'So Inter-Continental might be worth a try.'

'Oh, bother! That's my unfavourite one. Shall I be copped if I park here? Oh dear me, yes, just look at it! The whole place absolutely ringed with policemen. Can't you use your influence, Robin?'

'No, I'll do better than that. I'll drive it round to a car park for you. You and Tessa go in and get yourselves a bun. I'll find you upstairs.'

'What was Digby's part?' Toby asked again, when we had found a vacant bench in the Arrivals section. 'Or don't you know.'

'Yes, I do, but it wasn't a very heroic one. Digby was a mere tool.'

'Who for?'

'His brother. Before she got around to the implications of it, Betsy had been dropping hints that Maud's tape-recordings contained all sorts of scandalous indiscretions and Piers couldn't wait to get his hands on them. Unfortunately for him, as soon as Maud died Betsy saw the red light and locked them all away, pretending they'd been lost.'

'Very teasing of her!'

'Very much in character, though. Everything had to be sweetness and light in Betsy's life, with no unpleasantness such as libel suits to spoil things. Anyway, her covering-up manoeuvre didn't quite work out that time, because Piers came on the tapes quite by chance. He was looking for a dressing-gown for Sophie and he discovered that Betsy's wardrobe was locked. That must have put the bit between his teeth, because he forced it open and there they all were. However, he couldn't very well march downstairs carrying them in his arms and risk running slap into Betsy in the hall, so he had to make another plan. Never being one to do his own dirty work if it could be avoided, he collared Digby and passed on the instructions to him. After that he went back and sat with Sophie, presumably to shoo away anyone who might have come into the room, and also to ensure, if he could, that she was fast asleep before Digby came back with the ladder.'

'He was foiled, however?'

'Perhaps Sophie wasn't quite asleep, after all, and caught Digby in the act, or perhaps he lost his nerve at the last minute. Personally, I think it was foolhardy of Piers to leave the job to him. He's obviously destined to go through life making a hash of everything he touches.'

'Anyway, that clears up the mystery of the tape recordings?'

'Well, not quite, because there was still one tin unaccounted for, which Betsy knew nothing about, and that was the one Albert had swiped in advance. It had nothing to do with Maud's scandalous revelations, what's more.'

'Really, Tessa, you have been busy! No wonder the mere sight of you was beginning to get on Jasper's nerves. It surprises me that you didn't get shut in a linen cupboard yourself.'

'Oh, I expect I'd have been next in line. He was getting well into his stride in mowing down anyone who stood in his path: but it was first things first and Albert presented the main threat at that time.'

'Because Jasper's voice was on the same tape with Maud dictating her new will to Gerald? Isn't that your theory?'

'It was once upon a time, but I've changed my mind since then. As Robin pointed out, it wouldn't have proved conclusively that he'd overheard the lot. No, I think this one contained a far more damaging piece of evidence, and it was probably recorded weeks ago, before everyone got into the habit of remembering that Maud was liable to leave it switched on, whether she was using it or not. And can you guess what was on it, Toby?'

'No, but I'm sure you would love to tell me and stun me with your cleverness, so you have my permission to do so.'

'It wasn't all that clever; more a stroke of luck, because I had sources of information which were denied to poor old Mackenzie, and one of them was Mr Jackie.'

'There now, you've done it! I am veritably stunned.'

'Yes, but you see, one of the most puzzling elements and one which none of us ever concentrated on enough was what made Maud change her will at all and leave everything to Betsy? None of them expected it, least of all Betsy herself, and that tight-lipped Margot was so utterly fazed that she lost all control and behaved in a most unladylike fashion. So obviously she had nothing on her conscience, and the question remained: why had Maud done it?'

'I hope you're not asking me to believe that Mr Jackie supplied the answer?'

'Only inadvertently, but he showed me how Jasper could have gone to work. Getting the will changed in Betsy's favour was the first move in his game and, once he'd accomplished that, everything else followed. Did you know that Maud was practically bald?'

'No, I can't say I did.'

'Nor did anyone else, except Betsy and Mr Jackie. It was a closely guarded secret and Maud would have broken off relations instantly, if either of them had given it away.

But, you see, Toby, just recently there must have been one other person who knew all about it.'

'We're back with the dreaded Maureen?'

'Yes. That would be one secret you couldn't keep from a nurse, wouldn't it? Specially a night nurse.'

'And Maureen passed the news on to Jasper?'

'Right. It was all he needed.'

'Oh, come, come, Tessa! You're not telling me that he marched up to her and said: "I know it's a wig and unless you change your will and leave it all to my wife I shall ring up the *Daily Express* this very minute"?'

'No, not at all; nothing so crude. It so happens that Margot goes to the same hairdresser. All Jasper had to do was to tell Maud that he'd heard about her secret from some acquaintance in London and that Margot was giving out the news at every party she went to and getting a great big laugh, etc.'

'Well, you astound me. What a caddish trick! Really, I begin to feel quite glad they've caught him. One could never say where that kind of thing would end.'

'And I bet he got a great kick out of dealing Maudie such a death blow and doing Margot down in the same stroke. He always hated her and he was terribly spiteful.'

'Poor old Margot! Still we don't mind too much about her, do we?'

'Not too much, no.'

'Robin's taking his time, isn't he? I hope he hasn't been arrested.'

'More likely spinning it out on purpose. He's heard it all before and we have to remember that, however enthralling to you and me, all this kind of thing is rather a busman's holiday for him.'

'I expect you're right. Did Albert realise that this charming conversation had been recorded, and use it for blackmail?'

'Correct. He'd trained himself to be rather more observant, in small ways, than the average person. He may have overheard part of it and, when he realised the machine had been running, he pinched the tape and kept it for a rainy day. Unfortunately he couldn't play it back on Maud's machine, because Margot had chucked that out during her transports of grief, but on the day of the funeral, when everyone was safely occupied elsewhere, he concealed it in a bunch of flowers and took it over to the Stables, knowing that Jasper's workshop was piled high with every sort of recording device. And how he must have congratulated himself on picking up such a little gem! Poor Albert! Not a very noble character, but personally I'd say he'd been punished enough. It can't have been much fun, shut up in that ghastly linen cupboard and knowing it might be days or even weeks before anyone found you. Even if his wife had got worried, she'd have been reluctant to drag the police in, seeing what they'd both been up to all these years.'

'So it wasn't true about their being separated?'

'Oh no, but they hadn't time to cover their tracks when Maud died so unexpectedly. Their one thought was to grab what they could while the going was good. I imagine Albert threw in that yarn about his wife's elopement because, misjudging her so completely, he believed some hard luck story was needed to soften Betsy's heart if the truth came out about his thefts and so on. The Devonshire bit was pure invention. She never got further than a housing estate in Storhampton, but Ted Williams kept a tobacco shop just around the corner from the houses where they'd salted away their ill-gotten gains. They knew he'd done a flit and they used it to build up their story.'

'Honestly, Tessa, you amaze me sometimes. How did you find all that out?'

'It was one of several items which were tossed into my lap by Owen the Taxi. Another was that local opinion had it that Betsy committed suicide. Owen, who's a bit of a puritan, said it was excusable in view of all she had to put up with. I knew he couldn't be referring to Jasper's usual line of squalid infidelities, because people had got quite used to those. It had to be something far more serious. As a matter of fact, Mrs Chalmers dropped a fairly broad hint on the subject, only like a fool I didn't take it up. She was talking about Maureen and she said she wondered Mrs Craig didn't put her foot down. I thought she was referring to Piers, but she's a pretty bright female and she'd obviously realised that Jasper was Maureen's real target.'

'The plane landed ten minutes ago,' Robin announced, taking his seat on the bench, 'so they should be through quite soon. Well, Toby, have you heard the whole saga now?'

'Yes. Tessa is flushed with triumph.'

'I can add something to make her cheeks rosier still. It's the accolade, Tessa. Mackenzie claims to have had a sharp eye on Jasper right from the start and it was all on account of your telling him about that broken vine.'

'What broken vine?'

'The one you noticed hanging loose on the day before the funeral. It planted the idea that Jasper had the best opportunity for doing it.'

'How absolutely staggering, incredible and amazing!'

'Oh, I don't know. He may not be brilliant, but he's quite capable of putting two and two together.'

'He put two and nothing together this time. What I told him was quite untrue. I haven't the faintest idea whether the vine was broken then, or not. I invented it to get him to show his hand. It worked, and that's how I knew the balcony had been sawn through deliberately.'

'Ah! I see. Well, perhaps we won't tell him that.'

'Would you like to hear what really gave Jasper away?'

'Yes, of course,' they both replied dutifully.

'It was because Betsy would go on insisting that her Family Planners met on Wednesday, even when she knew damn well it wasn't true. That was so inconsistent because normally she'd have gone around telling everyone what a fool she was to have turned up at a meeting twenty-four hours late. Obviously, what happened was that she set out in good faith, realised her mistake when she got there and came home again. The front door was always left open, so she wouldn't have made any noise coming in, and what did she see as she stepped into the hall?'

'You win! What did she see?'

'Jasper, at the top of the stairs, with his ear to Maud's keyhole. He who was supposed to be out on the river with all cameras rolling. What he was actually doing, you may be sure, was listening in to Maud's conversation with Gerald, to make sure the new will was coming out the way he'd planned it. Until that was accomplished, he couldn't make the next move.'

'So Betsy, not knowing what it was all about, left him to it and went out of the house again?'

'Well, she must have realised he was engaged in something underhand. Being her, she wouldn't want to know, but I daresay it weighed on her terribly, and I'm sure it was mainly the cause of her being so worried and unhappy. Poor Betsy! Much as I shall miss her, I can't be altogether sorry that she died. She hadn't much to look forward to. So far as Jasper is concerned though, it just goes to show.'

'Look out!' Robin warned. 'Here comes the moral!'

'You're right, and the moral is that if Jasper hadn't been so megalomaniac and selfish, and had taken the slightest interest in Betsy's affairs, he'd have known that the Planners met on Tuesday and been on his guard. So it just goes to show that it's not in our stars, but in ourselves that we are unsuccessful murderers.'

'Oh God!' Toby said. 'Can it be true?'

He had ceased to listen to me and was staring in horror at the Customs exit. Two self-important-looking businessmen had just bustled through, followed by what appeared to be a female albino Bedouin. She was tanned to a mid-mahogany, her hair the colour of bleached bones, and she wore a flowing patchwork skirt, with bits of looking-glass stuck all over it. She carried, among other mystifying paraphernalia, a full size, filigree beehive.

'It's a birdcage,' she explained, setting it down on the bench, the better to fling herself into the arms of her startled relatives. 'Just what I need for my bedroom.'

'I got you some gorgeous brass earrings, Tessa,' she said, when it came to my turn, 'but unfortunately they were too heavy to pack.'

'I am relieved to hear it,' I replied. 'Too many people have been giving me jewellery just lately. It has led to no end of trouble and I'm all for making a fresh start.'

THE END

FELICITY SHAW

THE detective novels of Anne Morice seem rather to reflect the actual life and background of the author, whose full married name was Felicity Anne Morice Worthington Shaw. Felicity was born in the county of Kent on February 18, 1916, one of four daughters of Harry Edward Worthington, a well-loved village doctor, and his pretty young wife, Muriel Rose Morice. Seemingly this is an unexceptional provenance for an English mystery writer—yet in fact Felicity's complicated ancestry was like something out of a classic English mystery, with several cases of children born on the wrong side of the blanket to prominent sires and their humbly born paramours. Her mother Muriel Rose was the natural daughter of dressmaker Rebecca Garnett Gould and Charles John Morice, a Harrow graduate and footballer who played in the 1872 England/Scotland match. Doffing his football kit after this triumph, Charles became a stockbroker like his father, his brothers and his nephew Percy John de Paravicini, son of Baron James Prior de Paravicini and Charles' only surviving sister, Valentina Antoinette Sampayo Morice. (Of Scottish mercantile origin, the Morices had extensive Portuguese business connections.) Charles also found time, when not playing the fields of sport or commerce, to father a pair of out-of-wedlock children with a coachman's daughter, Clementina Frances Turvey, whom he would later marry.

Her mother having passed away when she was only four years old, Muriel Rose was raised by her half-sister Kitty, who had wed a commercial traveler, at the village of Birchington-on-Sea, Kent, near the city of Margate. There she met kindly local doctor Harry Worthington when he treated her during a local measles outbreak. The case of measles led to marriage between the physician and his patient, with the couple wedding in 1904, when Harry was thirty-six and Muriel Rose but twenty-two. Together Harry and Muriel Rose had a daughter, Elizabeth, in 1906. However Muriel Rose's three later daughters—Angela, Felicity and Yvonne—were fathered by another man, London playwright Frederick Leonard Lonsdale, the author of such popular stage works (many of them adapted as films) as *On Approval* and *The Last of Mrs. Cheyney* as well as being the most steady of Muriel Rose's many lovers.

Unfortunately for Muriel Rose, Lonsdale's interest in her evaporated as his stage success mounted. The playwright proposed pensioning off his discarded mistress with an annual stipend of one hundred pounds apiece for each of his natural daughters, provided that he and Muriel Rose never met again. The offer was accepted, although Muriel Rose, a woman of golden flights and fancies who romantically went by the name Lucy Glitters (she told her daughters that her father had christened her with this appellation on account of his having won a bet on a horse by that name on the day she was born), never got over the rejection. Meanwhile, "poor Dr. Worthington" as he was now known, had come down with Parkinson's Disease and he was packed off with a nurse to a cottage while "Lucy Glitters," now in straitened financial circumstances by her standards, moved with her daughters to a maisonette above a cake shop in Belgravia, London, in a bid to get the girls established. Felicity's older sister Angela went into acting for a profession, and her mother's theatrical ambition for her daughter is said to have been the inspiration for

Noel Coward's amusingly imploring 1935 hit song "Don't Put Your Daughter on the Stage, Mrs. Worthington." Angela's greatest contribution to the cause of thespianism by far came when she married actor and theatrical agent Robin Fox, with whom she produced England's Fox acting dynasty, including her sons Edward and James and grandchildren Laurence, Jack, Emilia and Freddie.

Felicity meanwhile went to work in the office of the GPO Film Unit, a subdivision of the United Kingdom's General Post Office established in 1933 to produce documentary films. Her daughter Mary Premila Boseman has written that it was at the GPO Film Unit that the "pretty and fashionably slim" Felicity met documentarian Alexander Shaw—"good looking, strong featured, dark haired and with strange brown eyes between yellow and green"—and told herself "that's the man I'm going to marry," which she did. During the Thirties and Forties Alex produced and/or directed over a score of prestige documentaries, including *Tank Patrol, Our Country* (introduced by actor Burgess Meredith) and *Penicillin*. After World War Two Alex worked with the United Nations agencies UNESCO and UNRWA and he and Felicity and their three children resided in developing nations all around the world. Felicity's daughter Mary recalls that Felicity "set up house in most of these places adapting to each circumstance. Furniture and curtains and so on were made of local materials. . . . The only possession that followed us everywhere from England was the box of Christmas decorations, practically heirlooms, fragile and attractive and unbroken throughout. In Wad Medani in the Sudan they hung on a thorn bush and looked charming."

It was during these years that Felicity began writing fiction, eventually publishing two fine mainstream novels, *The Happy Exiles* (1956) and *Sun-Trap* (1958). The former novel, a lightly satirical comedy of manners about British and American expatriates in an unnamed British colony during the dying days of the Empire, received particularly good reviews and was published in both the United Kingdom and the United States, but after a nasty bout with malaria and the death, back in England, of her mother Lucy Glitters, Felicity put writing aside for more than a decade, until under her pseudonym Anne Morice, drawn from her two middle names, she successfully launched her Tessa Crichton mystery series in 1970. "From the royalties of these books," notes Mary Premila Boseman, "she was able to buy a house in Hambleden, near Henley-on-Thames; this was the first of our houses that wasn't rented." Felicity spent a great deal more time in the home country during the last two decades of her life, gardening and cooking for friends (though she herself when alone subsisted on a diet of black coffee and watercress) and industriously spinning her tales of genteel English murder in locales much like that in which she now resided. Sometimes she joined Alex in his overseas travels to different places, including Washington, D.C., which she wrote about with characteristic wryness in her 1977 detective novel *Murder with Mimicry* ("a nice lively book saturated with show business," pronounced the *New York Times Book Review*). Felicity Shaw lived a full life of richly varied experiences, which are rewardingly reflected in her books, the last of which was published posthumously in 1990, a year after her death at the age of seventy-three on May 18th, 1989.

Curtis Evans

Printed in Great Britain
by Amazon

68876002R00121